Her breasts were the most marvelous I had seen since I left a girl named Sara in San Francisco, almost two years before.

As soon as the door to my room closed behind us she was in my arms, a wild thing with a raging fire going on somewhere deep inside her. My aim was to find that fire and quench it, no matter how long it took.

We disrobed and fell to the bed, locked in a tight embrace. There seemed to be acres and acres of her and it was all beautiful. She smelled fresh and sweet, and tasted even better.

Her lips were full and warm, her tongue alive as it found places on my body that I had not even been aware of. They had taught her more than you could get from a book during her stay back East, and I was getting the benefit of that learning.

THE GUNSMITH

7

THE LONGHORN WAR

J.R. Roberts

CHARTER
NEW YORK

A Division of Charter Communications Inc.
A GROSSET & DUNLAP COMPANY
51 Madison Avenue
New York, New York 10010

THE GUNSMITH #7: THE LONGHORN WAR
Copyright © 1982 by Robert J. Randisi

An Ace Charter Original
First Ace Charter printing: July 1982
Published simultaneously in Canada

Manufactured in the United States of America
2 4 6 8 0 9 7 5 3 1

THE GUNSMITH #7:
THE LONGHORN WAR

Dedication

This one is for my friend, Joseph Randisi, Jr., who also happens to be my brother.

From 1859 to 1872, Mexican bandits reportedly stole 145,298 cattle and 4,308 horses from ranches near the tip of Texas. These figures, however, do not even approach the number of stock stolen from the Mexicans by Texas ranchers who considered all Mexicans to be hostile, even those on the Texas side of the border.

Some Texans crossed the Rio Grande at night and swam large herds across to the Texas side.

This is where the term "wet stock" comes from.

Prologue

The hides of the "wet stock" glistened in the moonlight as the cattle swam across the Rio Grande from Mexico to Texas. This was not the first such drive across the river border, and it would certainly not be the last. As long as the Mexicans continued to steal stock from Texas, there would be reprisals, and on a much larger scale.

The man running this particular wet stock operation was Deke Bronson, a Texan born and raised, and it gave him special satisfaction to be in charge. He hated Mexicans, all Mexicans, even those little spitfires he crossed the river to bed down with now and then. They were good for an occasional screw, but that was all they were good for.

"How many head we get, Deke?" one of the men asked.

"Didn't count yet," he said, looking the cattle over with a practiced eye, "but I figure maybe seventy-five, eighty head. We could have done better."

He always said that. One night they had grabbed upwards of two hundred and fifty head, and he still muttered those same words.

When it came to stealing from Mexicans, he never got enough.

"Deke," the man asked, "what happened back there?

I heard shooting. Anybody get hurt?"

"None of our men," Deke Bronson said with satisfaction.

"Theirs?"

"A couple," Deke admitted. He thought back fondly to the moment he'd sent a .45-caliber slug rocketing through the head of one of those Mexican hands. Took the whole back of his head out clean as a whistle. He'd thrown a slug at another one, but didn't think he'd hit him bad enough to kill him. That was okay. He and his men always wore masks on their nocturnal cattle drives.

"Was it necessary?" the other man asked.

"You questioning my judgment, Cletus?" Deke asked the other man coldly.

Cletus Smith avoided his boss's glare and said, "No, boss, I ain't questioning you. I'm just curious, that's all."

"Well, stop being curious," Deke advised him, "and get these cattle moving!"

"Sure, Deke," Cletus said, and rode off to tell the rest of the men to speed them up.

Necessary, Deke Bronson thought, that was a laugh. When wasn't it necessary to kill a damn Mexican?

Lansdale, Texas
1873

1

The town of Lansdale, Texas was about as far south as you could get without actually being in the Rio Grande —or Mexico. I wasn't actually headed there, but was close enough so that changing my direction when the need arose was not a major inconvenience.

The reason that the need arose was a girl named Laura Kennedy. When I first saw her she was hunkered down behind her horse, inspecting a hoof, and I pulled my rig to a stop and began to inspect the hind portion of her jeans, which she filled out very nicely, thank you. I decided to go down and see if she needed any help, since I was in no particular hurry to get anywhere special.

She heard me as I rode up behind her, dropped the horse's hoof and turned, planting her hands on her hips. She was a big girl, this one, full in the breasts and hips, standing almost six feet in her bootheels. She appeared to be about twenty-two, but I was never especially good at guessing women's ages.

"You need any help, Miss?" I asked her.

The sun was at my back, so she squinted up at me and said, "Well, first of all, I'd be obliged if you'd step down from that wagon so I wouldn't have to fight the sun to see your face, Mister."

"My pleasure." I set the break and hopped down to

the ground. That was when I noticed how tall she was. "What seems to be the problem?" I asked her.

"My animal pulled up limping for some reason. I was just trying to find out why when I heard you pull up."

"Left hind leg?" I asked, approaching her horse, a young mustang colt who should have known better than to step on a stone.

"Yes."

I lifted his leg and sure enough, he had a nice stone bruise.

"Not too bad," I told her, "but he shouldn't be ridden."

She noticed Duke standing behind my wagon, untethered.

"My God," she exclaimed. Duke was a massive black gelding with more speed, stamina, and intelligence than any animal I'd ever seen. He was almost six, and I'd had him for five years.

She walked over to him and reached out a hand to stroke his nose, but he tossed his head to discourage her. That didn't bother her none. She walked on around him, continuing to examine him with a light in her eyes.

"That's Duke," I explained.

"What a mundane name for such a beautiful animal."

"Duke and I don't go in much for fancy names."

"Do you want to sell him?" she asked.

"No, Miss—"

"I'll give you a thousand dollars," she offered, coming back to face me again.

"You have that kind of money, ma'am?" I asked.

"My father's Enoch Kennedy. He owns one of the biggest spreads around these parts. In fact, you're on Kennedy land right now."

"Well, Miss, I'll tell you, I could no more sell Duke than cut off one of my arms."

"I'll make it fifteen hundred."

"You could make it fifteen thousand, Miss, I still wouldn't accept. Now, I'll be glad to give you a ride to wherever it is you want to go, but that's all."

She pressed her lips together in annoyance, then said, "All right. I'll take you up on your offer."

She looked back at Duke, and then asked me, "Could I ride him?"

"I'm afraid not, Miss. You see, he don't let anybody but me ride him."

"Nobody else has ever ridden him?" she asked.

"No, Miss."

"Stop calling me that. My name is Laura. Laura Kennedy."

"Well, Miss Kennedy, if you'll let me help you up onto the wagon, I'll tie your horse to the back and we can be off."

I helped her step up, tied up her horse, warned Duke about trying anything with the younger animal—the big boy could break another animal's spirit if he put his mind to it—and then joined Laura Kennedy up front.

"Where are we going?" I asked her. She smelled of horses and sweat, but her hair, which was long and reddish-brown, still smelled fresh and sweet.

"Lansdale is that way, a couple of hours ride. If you don't mind, it's closer than my father's ranch."

"Must be a big spread," I commented, impressed.

Conversation was scarce the first hour, and I got tired of being so close to the pretty woman without talking.

"You sound well-educated, Miss Kennedy," I commented.

"Call me Laura," she said.

"You can call me Clint."

"I was educated back East, Clint, but came back here to live when my schooling was completed. I love this country. There's room to breathe."

"I see," I said. I had been born in the East, but had
come West at an early age and had never returned.

"I think I love riding more than anything else," she
said. "When my horse started to limp, I was just riding,
enjoying the space."

"I know what you mean," I replied.

"You would, I guess," she said, "owning an animal
like that."

"I don't think of Duke as a possession, Miss—Laura.
We're more like friends. We travel together, take care of
each other. In fact, Duke is probably the best friend I've
got."

Hearing about the way I felt about Duke seemed to
bring some approval to her eyes. Not that she'd shown
any disapproval of me before that, but there had not
been any readable reaction in her eyes up to that point.
I'd scored a few points, and was glad of it. She was a big,
healthy young filly, and I was glad to see that I was
having some effect on her, at last.

"You love that horse, don't you?"

"Yes, I suppose I do."

"I'm sorry I sounded so stuffy back there, offering
you money for him."

"Don't apologize."

"Where are you from?"

"Originally, or within the last two days?" I asked.

"Originally."

"Back East. Came West when I was in my teens, on
my own."

"What have you done since?"

"This and that." I wasn't ashamed of being an ex-
lawman, but tell people that and they tend to get quiet
on you.

"What's in the wagon?" she asked.

"Tools," I told her. "Gunsmith tools."

"You're a gunsmith by trade?"

"I guess you could say that. Never went to school, or anything, I just sort of picked up the knowledge along the way. I fix them, sometimes I sell them. I like guns."

"I don't," she said. "They kill people."

"No gun ever killed anybody all by itself, Laura. There's always somebody behind it, pulling the trigger."

"I guess you could look at it that way," she said, unconvinced.

I decided not to try to change her mind.

"Is there anything else you like besides guns and horses?" she asked. I looked at her, but she was looking straight ahead and I couldn't read what was in her eyes. The question appeared to be innocent enough.

"I like a good meal, strong coffee, a soft bed every once in a while . . . and the company of a pretty lady."

I felt her look at me, but I kept my head straight so that she couldn't read anything in my eyes.

It was a perfectly innocent remark, though—like hell!

2

The town of Lansdale, Texas was probably the biggest town I had never heard of. Judging from its size, and the wealth of its activity, it deserved to be better known. I wondered why I had never heard of it.

"My father is the most important man in the territory, Clint," Laura explained. "He pays a lot of money to keep Lansdale *off* the map."

"Why?"

"Because he's a very private man," she said.

"Well, I guess if he can afford it."

"He can," she assured me.

I guessed Enoch Kennedy had his reasons for doing what he did, and questioned it no further.

When we got to town Laura gave me directions to the livery stable, then hopped down from the wagon.

"Thanks for the ride, Clint. A lot of people wouldn't have stopped," she said, "or would have stopped for different reasons."

"No problem," I told her.

"Will you be moving on?" she asked.

"I don't think so," I answered. "I think now that I'm here I might stay awhile—at least overnight."

I got down from the wagon and untied her horse for her. When the livery man came out, he greeted her by

11

name, and she told him what had happened.

"I'll be glad to take care of your hoss for you, Miss Laura," the old man said. He had about four teeth in his mouth, and smiled constantly.

"Take care of this man's property, Jake, and put it on my father's bill."

"That's not necessary, Laura."

"No, I insist. My father would want—"

"Laura, I would rather pay my own bills, if you don't mind," I said, firmly.

"Oh," she said. She seemed flustered, then said, "Well, I only wanted to thank—"

"If you want to thank me, you can do it another way," I told her.

She stared at me for a moment, and I thought I'd better clarify my remark before she drew the wrong conclusion.

"You can have dinner with me," I said. "That is, unless you're in a hurry to get back to the ranch."

"Dinner," she repeated, as she adjusted her thinking from what she might have thought I meant. Her face brightened with an idea of her own and she said, "I'll buy you dinner."

"No, no," I told her. "I will buy you dinner. If you say yes, that's all the thanks I need."

She thought it over for about two seconds and then said, "All right, yes."

"Good."

"Stay at the Kennedy hotel," she said. "I'll meet you there at seven."

"The Kennedy hotel?" I asked.

"It's my father's," she admitted, "but I'll insist that you pay your bill."

"Okay," I said, smiling.

"I'll see you later, Clint."

When she left I made my arrangements with the livery

man to put up my rig and team and take extra special care of Duke. As usual, that cost me a few extra bucks, but it was always worth it to me to see that the big boy was well taken care of.

I took my saddle bags and rifle and walked over to the Kennedy hotel. On the way I passed other stores—General Store, Hardware, and a number of others—bearing the Kennedy name. I wondered why the whole town wasn't named after Kennedy.

"How long?" the clerk asked as I was signing in.

"At least overnight, maybe longer," I told him.

"Mister, I gotta know how long," he started to say, then he stopped. "Hey, are you the Clint who helped out Miss Laura?"

"Yes, I am," I told him.

He checked the name again. "Clint Adams. Miss Laura said she forgot to ask you for your last name." He turned and took a key out of a box behind the counter.

"We have a very nice room for you, Mr. Adams. A suite." He handed me the key.

I left the key in his hand and said, "I don't need a suite. Have you got something on the second floor, overlooking the street?"

"Uh, yes, but it's not as nice," he told me, looking puzzled. He was a middle-aged man, short with a big belly on a skinny frame.

"It'll do," I assured him, taking the new key he was offering me. "Thanks."

"My pleasure, sir. If there is anything we can do to make your stay a comfortable one, please let us know."

"I will," I said. I started to walk away, then turned and said, "I'll try and let you know ahead of time when I'm checking out."

He put on a phony smile and said, "No problem, sir. Stay as long as you like."

I regarded him for a moment, then shook my head

and started up the stairs to the next floor. Laura Kennedy seemed intent on doing more than just having dinner with me to say thank you.

I wondered just how much she was really willing to do.

That was a ridiculous thought, I realized. As much as I would like her to offer me her body as thanks, it wasn't as if I had saved her life. All I did was save her a long walk.

Oh well, maybe that together with a nice dinner and some pleasant conversation would do the trick.

Then again, I thought, rubbing my hand over the stubble on my face, nothing would work if I didn't get a shave and a bath and make myself more presentable.

I stashed my gear in my room and went about doing whatever had to be done to make me irresistible to Laura Kennedy.

3

When I came out of the barber's, all shaved and bathed, I decided that a drink was in order, and a visit to the sheriff.

I tried to make it a rule to announce my arrival to the sheriff of any town I visited. I couldn't ignore the fact that my name was fairly well known throughout the West, and as an ex-lawman I understood the importance of knowing just about everyone who enters your town. It created good will between me and the town sheriff—in most cases.

Lansdale had several saloons, and I picked one at random. It wasn't the largest, but then I didn't want a very large drink, just something to lubricate my throat. I'd gotten all of the dust off the outside, now I wanted to clean the insides.

I went into the saloon and ordered a beer. When the bartender brought it back, he asked the inevitable bartender's question.

"Just get into town?"

"Yep."

"Passing through?"

"Yep."

"My name is Bill," he said, sticking out his hand. This was a new one on me. I'd met friendly bartenders in my time, but never this friendly.

I took his hand and he said, "Chambers, Bill Chambers."

Bill the bartender was about five-nine or so, husky and tough-looking, but wearing a friendly smile all the same.

"Clint," I told him.

"Clint," he repeated, and his tone said he was fishing for a last name.

"That's right," I said, and buried my nose in my beer.

"Uh, yeah," he said, "okay. Listen, uh, what's your business?"

"Mine," I said.

"Huh?"

"My business is my business."

"Oh, yeah, I get it. Okay, pal, forget it."

I continued to work on my beer and he drifted down the bar to tend to someone else's needs. I could see in the mirror behind the bar that the place was pretty busy, although it wasn't filled up. There was a table in a corner with three men sitting at it, and they seemed particularly interested in my back. A few minutes later, a fourth man walked in, sat down with them and started talking to the three of them. What he was saying seemed to be pretty important, and it appeared to have something to do with me.

By the time I finished my beer, they had made some kind of a decision, and one of them—the fourth man— stood up and came over to the bar.

As I put down my empty beer mug and paid for the beer, he came up next to me. When I turned to leave, he deliberately bumped into me.

"Hey, watch where you're going," he said in a nasty tone. He was about my height, a little heavier, with a droopy mustache and no chin.

"You bumped me, friend, and on purpose. What's the problem?"

"The problem is you, friend," he said. "My buddies over there and I would be happy if you would go to your hotel, pack your stuff, and leave town."

"Why would I want to do that?" I asked.

"Because we don't like gunslingers coming into town and messing around in private wars."

"Private wars?" I asked. "What are you talking about?"

He started to laugh and turned to his friends.

"He says he doesn't know what I'm talking about, Fred," he called over to them.

A man I assumed to be Fred stood up and, "Well, maybe we ought to refresh his memory a little."

The other two stood up and all three approached me, until I was encircled by them. They were all young and range-hard, but none of them was a gunman. If I tried to fight them I'd probably take a beating, but on the other hand I didn't have any desire to kill one or more of them.

"Look, fellas, you've got a burr under your saddle about something, but it can't be anything you'd want to get killed over. Let's talk about it, huh?"

"Man wants to talk, Vern. He don't want to fight," the man called Fred said to the man with no chin.

"Talk?" Vern asked, frowning. "Maybe he don't deserve the rep he's walkin' around with, boys. Maybe we ought to take it away from him."

I looked Vern right in the eye, because he seemed to be the man in charge, and told him, "If any of your friends makes a move I don't like, Vern, you're a dead man."

He held my eyes as long as he could, and then they started to play around the room.

"Think about it," I told him.

He was trying to think of a way of backing off without looking like he was backing off when a voice from the door said, "That's enough, boys. Back off."

I kept my eyes on Vern, watched him as his eyes looked towards the source of the voice.

"Sheriff," he said.

"Clear out," the voice from the door told them. "Now!"

"But Sheriff, this man is—" Fred started to say, but the stern voice cut him off.

"I know who the man is, Fred, and I'm telling you to back off. Vern, take Fred, Smith, and Williams and get out of here."

"Sure, Sheriff," Vern said, "whatever you say." He had to try one last display of false bravado, though. "You're lucky we're law abidin' citizens, pal. Think about what we said."

"What was it you said?" I asked, frowning. "I've forgotten already."

"That's it," the sheriff called out, before Vern could wrack his brain for a reply, "go on back to where you belong."

The four of them gave me long, lingering looks as they moved towards the door, and then they were out the door. I got my first opportunity to look at the sheriff.

If he had matched his voice, he would have been a big man in his forties, with a huge belly and old eyes, eyes that had seen it all.

Well, the eyes were there, but they were on a man barely thirty-five who wasn't even five and a half feet tall. His face was smooth, and looked younger than thirty-five, but his eyes added the extra years. He wore a Navy Colt on his hip and looked like he knew how to use it.

I suspected, however, that his most effective tool was

his voice, a deep, resonant bass that seemed to come up from somewhere deep inside of him and carried all the authority one voice could possibly carry.

"Sheriff," I said, "I'm glad to see you. I was just about to come over and talk to you."

"Is that a fact?" he asked. He looked around and eyed the table the four men had recently vacated. "Why don't we sit over there, then. Stopping killing is thirsty work."

"Fine with me," I agreed. "Beer?"

"Fine."

"Two beers," I told the bartender. When he set them on the bar I carried them over to the table and sat with the sheriff.

"My name's Cross," he told me, "Sheriff Amos Cross."

"My name's—"

"I know your name, Adams. I know who you are." He took a long pull at his beer.

"I assume they knew also," I said.

"They did."

"What was that all about, then? What did they mean about me messing in a private war."

"There's a small war going on hereabouts, Adams. It's not a full fledged range war, but it's building to that. You see, the biggest spread on this side of the river, and the biggest spread on the other side, appear to be stealing stock from each other. Cattle and horses."

"Can't you make an arrest?"

"I said they appear to be. I can't touch anybody on the other side. I have no jurisdiction there. I can't put my finger on any one man or group of men from this side who are crossing the border. They might even be doing it at night, for all I know."

"Crossing the border at night? And doing what, driving the stock right through the river to this side? Isn't that dangerous?"

"I guess it could be, yeah."

"Are we talking about Enoch Kennedy's spread?" I asked.

"We are. Ain't five other spreads combined that can match his for size. That was his daughter you brought into town earlier."

"I know. She told me."

"Want to tell me about that?"

"Nothing to tell. Her horse came up lame and I happened to pass by and gave her a ride."

"Just by coincidence?"

"By accident, is more like it."

"Oh, then you weren't headed this way?"

"If it weren't for her, Sheriff, I would have passed your town right by and never known it was here."

He nodded, and drank some more beer.

"Listen, who were those men, anyway? What makes them think I want part of any private war?"

"They're hands from the Kennedy ranch. When they heard you were in town, I guess they figured that you were on your way to see Martinez."

"Martinez? Who's he?"

"Victor Martinez. He owns the largest spread on the other side of the river. He and Kennedy have been going at it for years, but it's just in the last few months that each has been losing stock and accusing the other of stealing it."

"Why would they think I was working for Martinez?"

"You've got a reputation, Adams. I guess they figure if you was working for Kennedy they would have heard you were coming. The only other way they can figure it is that you're on your way south, to see Martinez. Either that, or he's having someone meet you here."

"I'm not here to meet anybody, Sheriff. I brought Miss Kennedy in as a favor, and then decided to stay awhile. I never heard of Lansdale."

"That's the way Mr. Kennedy likes it." He put his beer mug down empty and gave out a satisfied sigh. "You appear to be a right friendly fella, Adams. You always do favors for strangers?"

"As you say, Sheriff, I'm a right friendly fella. How'd they know who I was?"

He shrugged. "Got the word, I reckon, like I did."

"And how'd you get it?"

"Things have a way of getting around," was all he'd say.

"I guess the whole town knows by now?"

"I doubt it. I sort of nipped the word in the bud, you might say. Unless those boys pass the word, there aren't too many others who know about it, and I think they'll keep it quiet."

"Until they make another try for me?"

"Now, I'd hate for that to happen, Adams. I'd hate to see you kill any of those boys."

"Sheriff, I'd hate to see me kill anyone. The only reasons I would is to save myself some pain."

"Well, you used to be a lawman, Adams, so I'm gonna take you at your word and not relieve you of your gun." He stood up. "I run a quiet town. As long as you don't do nothing to change that, you're welcome to stay."

"Much obliged, Sheriff," I said.

"Stay out of trouble, Mr. Adams. That's all I ask."

"I'll do my best," I promised him.

He left and I sat and nursed my second beer. I was impressed with Amos Cross, but first impressions can be deceiving. For all I knew, he might be sitting snugly inside Enoch Kennedy's pocket, but I suppose that remained to be seen.

It wasn't hard to figure out how Vern and his friends got the word on me. They worked for Kennedy, and so did the clerk at the hotel. The only other one who knew

who I was was the sheriff, which could mean that he also
worked for Kennedy, but I was willing to give the man
the benefit of the doubt.

For now.

4

After the afternoon incident in the saloon, I hadn't really expected Laura Kennedy to show up, but she surprised me. When I answered the knock on my door, there she was. She had changed out of her riding clothes. She still wore pants and a shirt, but the shirt was silk, and the pants were not range jeans. I couldn't help wondering how she would have looked in a dress, though.

"You look surprised," she said.

"I am."

"You didn't think I'd show?" she asked. "Why?"

"I'll explain at dinner," I said, stepping out into the hall next to her.

"Aren't you going to invite me in?" she asked.

I shook my head. "That wouldn't be proper, and besides, I'm ready to go."

My clothes couldn't touch hers for quality, but at least they were clean.

"This is your town," I said. "Where do we eat?"

"There's a very good restaurant down the street," she answered. "They have a remarkably wide assortment of meals, and they're all delicious."

"Sounds fine."

And it was more than fine, it was superb. I hadn't had

a meal that approached it since San Francisco, and I mentioned it.

"The chef comes from San Francisco," she told me. "Father had him brought out here."

"This is your father's restaurant?" I asked.

"Yes, it is. Do you mind?"

"Not as long as I pay."

She frowned and studied my face. "You're a strange man. You didn't take the room I had held for you at the hotel."

"I'm comfortable where I am."

"Tell me why you were surprised I showed up."

"You don't know?" I asked.

"No, I don't."

I explained that I had been approached by some of her father's ranch hands and advised to leave town. I said that the arrival of the sheriff on the scene might have saved her father the problem of having to hire some new men.

"You sound pretty sure of yourself," she said. "Wasn't there any chance you might have gotten killed?"

"There's always a chance, Laura, but it wasn't very likely. At most I might have suffered a little pain, but that was all. They were just ranch hands, not gunmen."

"And you're a gunman?"

I put my coffee cup down very deliberately and said, "Why don't we stop playing games, Laura, all right?"

"All right, Clint," she agreed.

"Now, the desk clerk didn't look like he recognized my name, but it's pretty obvious that he did. I know he passed it on to your father's men, and probably to the sheriff. He must have passed that information on to you, as well."

She remained silent for a moment, and then said. "Yes, he did tell me who you were."

"Then you know what I am—or was—as well as who."

"As a matter of fact, I know most of what there is to know about you, Clint. The newspaper has a file on you."

"Your father owns the newspaper?"

"Yes, he does. I've been authorized to offer you an enormous amount of money to work for my father, Clint."

"You've been in contact with your father?" I asked.

She smiled. "Father had a telegraph line strung from town right to our house. He likes to be in touch at all time."

"I see." Suddenly I was struck by a great desire to meet Enoch Kennedy. "What does your father want me to do, Laura?"

"I would think that was obvious."

"I'll listen to your father's offer, but only from him, personally."

"That could be arranged, Clint," she said. "I'll take you out to the ranch tomorrow."

"Do you think you could keep your father's men from trying to kill me tonight, so I can get a good night sleep?"

"I think I can do that," she said, and there was a funny twinkle in her eyes. "As a matter of fact, I can do better than that," she said, rising to her feet. "I can act as your personal bodyguard."

"All night?" I asked.

5

Her breasts were the most marvelous I had seen since I left a girl named Sara in San Francisco, almost two years before. They were firm and smooth and had the added attraction of a light dusting of freckles in the slope between them.

As soon as the door to my room closed behind us she was in my arms, a wild thing with a raging fire going on somewhere deep inside her. My aim was to find that fire and quench it, no matter how long it took.

We disrobed and fell to the bed, locked in a tight embrace. My tongue found her large, brown nipples and teased them to life. She moaned and mashed my face tightly against her chest. There seemed to be acres and acres of her, and it was all beautiful. She had bathed since coming off the trail and she smelled fresh and sweet, and tasted even better.

Her lips were full and warm, her tongue alive as it found places on my body that I had not even been aware of. They had taught her more than you could learn from a book during her stay back East, and I was getting the benefit of that learning.

Finally, she brought her hips up to meet me and I entered her in one clean, piercing stroke. She caught her breath and then began to move her hips in unison with mine. We went slow, enjoying every delicious stroke to the fullest, and then suddenly she was a frenzy of activity beneath me. Her hands were all over, pulling at my buttocks, scratching my back, cupping my head. Her mouth was alive on my face as she continued to experience spasm after spasm. I could feel her belly trembling against mine. Finally she locked her legs around my waist, caught me in one last hip-grinding stroke, and then went limp beneath me.

As I started to withdraw she said, "No, don't leave," and continued to hold me tightly to her.

"I don't want to crush you," I told her.

"Mmm," she said against my mouth, "crush me. I'm a big girl, I can take it."

"This wasn't necessary, Laura. I mean, if you did it as thanks, or as incentive to work for your father—"

"Don't be a fool, Clint Adams," she told me. My remarks did not anger her in the least. "I did it because I wanted to, and because, if I didn't do it now, I might never get another chance again."

"Oh?" I said, raising my head so I could look at her lovely face. "And why is that?"

"Well, if you listen to my father's offer tomorrow," she explained, "and then you say no, he'll have no choice but to assume that you came here to work for Martinez."

I waited for her to finish, and when she didn't I said, "Yes? And?"

She kissed me again, long and deep, before continuing. "If that happens, Clint dear, he'll have no other choice than to have you killed."

If she expected me to be shocked at the statement, she was disappointed.

"Doesn't that bother you?" she asked.

"People have tried to kill me before, Laura," I told her. "I'm still here."

"Yes," she said, wiggling her hips, bringing me back to life inside of her, "I can tell that."

6

"Father will probably offer to buy your horse," Laura said the next morning, as we rode to her ranch.

"You already did," I replied.

"I know."

"I said no."

"I know."

"Didn't you tell him that?"

"You can't have a whole conversation over a telegraph wire, silly," she told me. "When he sees the horse, he's going to offer to buy him, it's that simple."

"Well, I'm going to say no, it's that simple."

"He'll offer you a lot of money," she warned me.

I looked over at her, astride a bay mare loaned to her by the livery man, and said, "The answer will still be no."

"I know that, too."

"Laura, what's your father's spread called?"

"The brand reads 'EK.' People usually call it the Kennedy spread."

"What's your father call it?"

She hesitated a moment, then said, "He named it after my mother. Actually, nobody calls it that but him."

"Calls it what?"

She looked embarrassed and turned her head so that

31

I could only see her profile when she said, "Laurietta."

There was a catch in her voice when she said her mother's name.

"Beautiful name."

"She was a beautiful woman."

We rode in silence for a few moments, and then it got too heavy to bear—for me. I could just imagine what it must have been like for her.

"How old were you when she died?" I asked.

She looked at me and said, "Five. That was eighteen years ago, when father was building the Kennedy spread. The house was finished, he had gotten his stock, hired all the men he needed—at that time just a handful —when mother took sick and died. My father was devastated and from that day on, whenever he refers to the ranch, he calls it 'Laurietta.' "

"Sounds like a beautiful tribute," I said.

For a moment I thought she wasn't going to answer, but when she did I was surprised at her vehemence.

"It's sick!" she snapped. "It cheapens my mother's name. She was a beautiful woman. I was only five, but I remember her as if I saw her yesterday. To name a collection of cows, horses, and dirt after her is . . . is. . . ." She couldn't think of an appropriate word, so she lapsed back into silence.

The ranch looked like it should have a moat around it, like one of those English castles I'd read about.

"Father just keeps adding rooms," Laura said as we dismounted. "I think he expects me to get married and fill them."

"Any chance of that happening?" I asked.

"Take good care of that black," she told the man who was leading Duke away. She turned to me and said, "Marriage? Sure, someday, but not in the near future. Unless. . ." she trailed off, giving me the eye.

"Uh, let's go see your father," I said quickly.

"Come on, coward," she said, putting her arm through mine.

She walked me through the front door into a large room filled with overstuffed chairs and skinny tables she called "antiques." They all looked pretty well preserved to me.

"Pour yourself a drink, Clint. I'll tell father you're here." She pointed to a small table with glass decanters on it and left.

I went over to the bottles, opened one, took a whiff, and then closed it. That stuff was too good to drink. A guy could get used to it.

Likewise the furniture. The chairs were too nice to sit in, and I spent my time waiting on my feet.

"Clint," Laura said when she returned. "Father will see you in his study."

"All right."

I followed her down a long hallway to a pair of double-doors. The house and the situation reminded me of another time in another house, in Mexico.

Enoch Kennedy sat behind a massive desk cluttered with everything but paper. The walls were covered with guns—old guns, new guns. I kind of hoped the old man and I would get along, so I could get a closer look at some of them.

"Father, this is Clint Adams," Laura introduced me. "Clint, my father, Enoch Kennedy."

"Mr. Kennedy," I said.

"That's all, Laura," the old man said, dismissing his daughter. Laura, like a dutiful little girl, turned and left me alone with her father.

Kennedy stood up, although it was kind of hard to tell. He was about the same size as the sheriff, and about twenty-five years older. The hair on his head was slate gray, what there was of it. There was a bald patch right at the crown, and there was a thatch of hair on his chin that would have filled it perfectly. He was skinny, just plain skinny, but you knew that if he was in a room with a hundred other people, ninety-nine of them would be looking at him, looking to please him.

I didn't like his first words. "You did my daughter a service, Mr. Adams, and I'm grateful for it, but that doesn't mean I won't plow you under if I find out you're working for Victor Martinez," he warned me.

"With all due respect, Mr. Kennedy," I replied, "who I work for is my business, and you've got nothing to say about it."

He gave me a long, hard stare and when I didn't wither under it he changed his tactics.

"All right, Adams, maybe I come on too strong. Will you have a drink?"

"No."

"Have a seat, then," he invited, and sat back down. I sat in a straight-backed chair with so much cushion that it would have been fought over in a bar.

"I want to hire you, Adams."

"And if I'm working for Martinez?"

"Then I want to hire you away from him. I'll—I *would* pay you double the amount he's paying you—and in American money."

He said the last two words as if they alone should cause me to accept his offer. I was struck at that moment by the absence of any Mexican flavor at all in a house so close to the Rio Grande. Enoch Kennedy seemed to be some kind of a super-American, a fanatic. And fanatics were dangerous.

"That would be a tempting offer, Mr. Kennedy, if I was for hire, but I'm not. Not by you, not by Victor Martinez, not by anybody."

"I'd like to believe you, Adams, but a man like you always has his reasons for riding into any town."

"I brought your daughter, remember?"

"You just happened to cross her path?"

"I never heard of your town, Mr. Kennedy. I hear you pay a lot of money to keep it that way, so that shouldn't be so hard for you to believe."

He thought about it.

"While you're thinking about that, you better tell your men to stay away from me, or you're liable to lose a couple."

"What's that mean?"

I told him about the incident in the saloon.

"What were their names?" he asked.

I thought a moment, not about Vern, he was easy to remember, but about the rest.

"Vern, a skinny guy with a droopy mustache, he was the man in the lead. The others were Fred, and a couple of quiet boys called Smith and Williams."

"I'll take care of them, Adams. I didn't send them after you, and if I did send someone after you, it wouldn't be four cowpokes."

"You got hired guns on your payroll, Mr. Kennedy. What do you need me for?"

"No gunmen work for me," he said. "I'm not looking for a shooting war, but if Martinez wants it that way, I'll match him gun for gun."

"Why don't you tell me what the story is, Mr. Kennedy? What's going on between you and Martinez?"

"If you don't work for either of us, what goes on between us is our business," he told me. "If you're not interested in it, Mr. Adams, then stay out of my way."

"Are you telling me to leave town?" I asked him.

"By no means. Whether you leave or stay is your business. I'm just saying that if you decide to stay, don't get in my way, because—"

"—you'll plow me under if I do. You said that before."

"And I meant it. I may not have a gun on my ranch

that can match yours, but I can get one."

"That's doubtful," I said modestly. There were plenty of guns around that were as good as mine, and undoubtedly some better, but there was no point in letting him know that I knew that.

My remark stopped him for a moment, and he had to work up a new head of steam.

"I could put so many guns in front of you that one of them would have to get to you," he said, revising his threat.

"You'd lose an awful lot of men that way, Kennedy," I told him. "Why all the threats, anyway?"

"I don't want you working for Martinez, Adams."

"I'm not."

"Well don't," he said. "Think of my daughter."

"What about her?" I asked, frowning.

"She's fond of you," he said. "If you worked for Martinez, it would hurt her."

"I didn't like you when I came in, Mr. Kennedy," I told him, "and I like you even less, now."

I got up and headed for the door. I was in such a hurry to get away from him that I even ignored the guns on the walls.

"Remember what I said, Adams!" he shouted behind me. I waved a hand at him and kept right on going until I was out the front door.

"Where's my horse?" I asked the cowboy who'd taken him from me.

"I'll get him for you."

The door opened behind me and for a moment I thought maybe the old man had followed me out, but it was Laura. She came trotting down the steps towards me.

"Clint, what happened?"

"Your father and I didn't get along."

"Did he offer you a lot of money?"

"We didn't get into figures," I replied. "I couldn't stay in the same room with him that long."

"He does tend to fill a room," she said.

"With a stench."

"Clint!"

"Come on, Laura, don't get all indignant on me. You don't like him all that much yourself."

Her shoulders stiffened and her jaw came up and she said, "He's still my father."

"That's your problem," I told her as the man came back with Duke. "I'll be in town for a while," I said, although I didn't know why. "At the hotel, if you want to talk to me."

She started to speak, and then stopped herself and just watched me as I mounted up.

"I won't be there all that long, though," I added, "so make up your mind quick."

I liked her, maybe too much. Maybe that's what was going to keep me in town longer than was good for me.

Maybe that was what would almost get me killed.

7

I was halfway between town and the ranch, about the same distance from the Rio Grande, when they picked me up. They came up on me fast, five of them, all spread out as if they knew what they were doing.

Only one of them had his gun out, but all it took was one.

They were all Mexican, and it didn't take a genius to figure out who they worked for.

"You will come with us, Señor," the man with the gun said. He was thin, like Vern, but his mustache was a tiny thing, barely discernible on his upper lip, and he wore a floppy sombrero. The others all stared at me blankly, as if they didn't understand English.

"Sure," I said. "Why not, since you asked so nicely. Are we going to see Martinez?" I asked.

"You will come with us, and not talk, please."

"Is it a long ride?"

"A man with an animal such as yours should not worry about taking long rides, Señor. We will be there soon. Andale!" he said, making a jerky motion with his gun.

Two of them took the lead, two rode behind, and the fifth man, the one with the gun, rode alongside me. If I made a move for him, one of the men behind me would blow me out of the saddle.

They hadn't even bothered to take my gun, but I had no plans to go for it, and they probably knew it. In fact, the man next to me holstered his after a while, and we just rode along like six pals.

I was interested in hearing Martinez's offer, not that I planned on taking him up on it, but it didn't hurt to listen.

Once we crossed the border into Mexico it was barely an hour's ride to Martinez's rancho. It was large, but nowhere as imposing as Kennedy's house. Still, I liked it better. It had more old world class than Kennedy's palace.

"Nice place," I commented to my five companions, but none of them chose to answer.

We rode up to the front door and the leader of the pack said, "Step down, please."

I did as he asked and the others dismounted, too. One of them took Duke's reins and I said, "Take good care of him."

"Muy bonito," the man said. I looked at the leader and he said, "Juan thinks your animal is very beautiful."

"Tell Juan thank you, but warn him not to try and ride him, or he'll find out how vicious my big friend can get."

He relayed my message to Juan, who looked at me dubiously. I nodded to him, to indicate that I wasn't joking, and he gingerly led Duke away. If he tried to ride him, Duke would probably toss him twenty feet. Hell, if he tried to pet him, he'd lose his hand.

"Inside, please," the leader said.

"What's your name?" I asked.

He thought a moment, then shrugged as he realized it would do no harm to tell me. "Esteban."

"Okay, Esteban, lead the way. Let's see what your boss has to say for himself."

Esteban led me into the house and told me, "Wait."

"I'm not going anywhere," I told him.

He left the room, which was quite different from the one I'd waited for Kennedy in. There was a bottle of tequila on a table with a dirty glass. It wasn't particularly a favorite of mine, but my throat was dry and I poured myself a glass. There were no lemons or salt, so I just tossed it down and waited while it burned its way to my stomach.

"I see you appreciate good tequila, Señor," a voice said.

I turned but didn't answer him right away, because my vocal chords hadn't recovered from the shock yet.

The man I assumed to be Victor Martinez appeared to be in his early fifties, with slicked-down black hair and a well cared for mustache. It wasn't as long as Vern's, but it was certainly larger than Esteban's—who had disappeared, by the way, leaving me with his boss, who was not armed.

Martinez was not alone, however. Standing next to him was a girl. She had dark skin and fiery eyes, lots of wild black hair, full lips and small, perfectly rounded breasts barely contained by a tight, low cut peasant blouse.

She had all of my attention, and she knew it. She raised one eybrow and looked me up and down.

"Sparks," Victor Martinez said.

"I beg your pardon?" I asked.

"When I see a man and a woman look at each other the way you and my daughter are right now, I see the sparks as they fly across the room. Poof! Sparks."

"Victor Martinez, I assume?" I said.

"Ah, por favor, Señor, I am sorry. I did not introduce myself. I am Victor Martinez, and this is my daughter, Lita."

"Lita?"

"Actually, her name is Estralita, but for some reason she prefers to be called Lita."

"I do not like my name," she said.

"Hush, child, it was your mother's name as well, and she bore it proudly. Go and fetch another bottle of tequila. Por favor, Señor Adams, pour yourself another drink, and one for me, as well."

"I've only got one glass," I told him.

"No problem, Señor. Pour yourself a drink and hand me the bottle."

He laughed and approached me, holding his hand out for the bottle. I poured myself some of the liquid and gave him the bottle. He upended it and let the clear liquor flood into his throat and then lowered the bottle with a contented sigh.

"Please, Señor, sit down," he said. The chair was plain, wooden chairs, unlike the ones in Kennedy's house.

"I regret that my furnishings are not as fancy as those of Señor Kennedy, but I would match my daughter against his at any time, eh? Don't you think so?"

"Ah, they are both very lovely girls," I said.

"And about the same age, too, I believe," Victor Martinez said. "Did he offer you his daughter?"

"I beg your pardon?" I asked.

"Among all the other things he must have offered you to work for him, did he offer you his daughter?"

"No, he didn't. In fact, I didn't give him a chance to offer me very much. I walked out on him."

He stared at me for a moment with a surprised look on his face, and then started laughing uproariously. At that moment Lita entered the room carrying a bottle of tequila that was three-quarters full.

"What is so funny, Papa?" she asked.

He said something to her in Spanish, and I assumed

he was telling her what I had just told him. She started laughing, also.

"I wish I could have been there to see his face," Martinez said, finally. He took another healthy drink from the bottle and emptied it, and in virtually the same motion flipped it away and took the other bottle from his daughter.

"A glass, Lita, por favor. I don't think Señor Adams is well enough acquainted with me to drink from the same bottle."

I didn't answer, and she dutifully went to get a glass for her father.

"I want you to work for me, Señor Adams, and if you attempt to walk out on me, I will shoot you."

"You don't have a gun," I said.

He looked down at himself in surprise and said, "Madre de dios, you noticed! Ah, so much for my bluff, eh?"

"Make your offer, Señor Martinez. I came to listen."

"You came because my men brought you," he said, as if he expected me to argue the point.

"Have it your way," I told him.

He frowned because I would not argue, and then he smiled expansively and said, "No matter. I will offer you a lot of money, Señor. American money, if you like. And with it, I will offer you my daughter."

"For what purpose?" I asked. "Marriage?"

He laughed. "For whatever purpose you wish."

Suddenly I didn't like him any better than I liked Enoch Kennedy.

"I don't think so, Señor," I told him.

"You haven't heard how much money I would offer," he said.

"I am not interested."

"You are a strange man. You have a reputation with

a gun. Such men are always after money."

"Don't judge me by my reputation, Martinez, and I won't judge you by your manner here today."

"What does that mean?" he asked.

"Your English is much better than you'd like me to believe, and I doubt that you are as crude as you make out. You probably figured that if I was put off by Kennedy's fancy trappings, you could win me over by being more down to earth. I told Kennedy and I'll tell you, I have no desire to get mixed up in your private war, not for money . . . or love."

"What is this about love?" Lita asked, as she came back into the room with a glass.

He waved a hand at her in annoyance and she lapsed into silence and listened.

"As you say in your country, we will drop the crap, Adams. If you work for Kennedy, you're going to get killed."

"That's funny. He told me the same thing about working for you. I'll tell you what I told him. Who I work for is my business, and threats from either one of you won't influence my decision, which is not to work for either of you."

"Why are you here, then?"

"You said it was because your men brought—"

"I mean why are you in Lansdale, Texas?" he asked, again showing annoyance.

"I helped Laura Kennedy when she was stranded with a lame horse. That's all there is to it. I've never heard of Lansdale, and thought I'd stick around awhile."

"I am to believe that your presence is just a coincidence, then?" he asked.

"You can believe whatever you like, Martinez. I'd like to get back to town before dark, so if you don't mind."

"Yes," he said, "I do mind." I stared at him and he suddenly smiled, slipping back into his former role. "I would be honored if you would share my roof tonight. You can leave for town in the morning. Riding in unfamiliar country can be dangerous at night. I wouldn't want anything to happen to you."

"Neither would I. In fact, I'm always very careful that nothing happens to me."

"That sounds like a threat, Señor Adams," he said.

"It's not, Señor Martinez. It's a simple statement of fact. Take it as that, and no more."

"As you wish," he sighed. "Lita will show you to your room, Señor. If you have a need for anything, you have but to ask. You are a guest in my house."

For want of something better to say, I said, "Thank you."

8

Lita showed me to a room and did not speak. She opened the door, let me in, and then left. There was a basin and pitcher and I cleaned up, undressed, and lay down on the bed. Darkness had fallen by then, and it was early. I was tired, but not sleepy. I started going over my options in my mind.

I could work for Kennedy, and have Martinez out to kill me.

I could work for Martinez, and have Kennedy out to kill me.

I could work for neither man, and possibly have both of them out to kill me.

I could move on.

The last made more sense by far, so why didn't I just move on? Was it curiosity? Boredom? Laura Kennedy?

After a while I started to get sleepy and turned down the lamp. I was just drifting off when the door opened and someone slipped into the room. My gunbelt was on the bedpost and I put my hand on my gun.

"You will not need the gun, Señor," she said softly. She slid the covers back and got into bed with me. She was nude, and her flesh was hot. "That is, unless you want me to leave," she added. "Then you will need the gun, for I have no desire to leave."

I turned to face her and I felt her breath on my face.
"Did your father send you?"

"No, Señor. I came because of the sparks."

I knew what she meant, and I believed her. I kissed
her and her mouth opened wide, as if she were intent on
swallowing me whole. Her hands snaked between us and
took hold of me, stroking me gently. Her touch was
feathery. Her mouth tasted of tequila and spice. Her
nipples were scraping my chest and I reached down and
took them into my mouth one at a time. As I sucked on
them she began to chant something in Spanish, over and
over, and her feathery touch on me became heavier.

I was about ready, but she beat me to it. With surpris-
ing strength for a small girl she rolled me over onto my
back, sat astride me and guided me to the slick lips of
her sex. With a great sigh she hovered above me, and
then came crashing down, swallowing me up and grind-
ing herself against me. I reached around and cupped her
buttocks and she began to slide me in and out of her. I
just lay there, letting her do all the work, and she
grunted with the effort and the pleasure of it. All the
while she murmured and chanted in Spanish, and I
didn't understand a word of it. When the words began
to catch in her throat I knew she was near her time.
When she started to cry, I knew she was ready and I let
myself go. She fought back a scream as our juices
mingled and she beat on my chest with tiny fists. I barely
felt it, though, so intense were the other sensations I was
experiencing.

After a few moments she lay on top of me and sought
my lips, biting my tongue with sharp, tiny teeth. Her lips
began to work their way about my face. They were very
soft, and her breath was very hot and coming in short
gasps as I started to grow again inside her.

"Madre de dios," she murmured when she felt me
stiffening inside of her. Slowly she moved her hips again,

and I matched her movements. When she speeded up, I speeded up, when she slowed down, I slowed down, and then I got tired of letting her have her way.

I grabbed her buttocks tightly and her breath caught in her throat at the pressure. I knew that when I released them my finger marks would still be there. Roughly, I turned her over and got on top of her without breaking contact. Once I was on top I began to control the tempo of my thrusts, and went wild. She began to buck and writhe beneath me, but I continued pounding. By morning she was going to be plenty sore, but she'd be plenty satisfied as well.

"Dios, dios. . ." she said, saying each word in time to my thrusts. Suddenly she was struck speechless and I knew it was time to let myself go again. She wrapped her arms and legs around me and milked me for all I was worth, biting on my shoulder the whole time so she wouldn't scream. A small part of my mind decided that her father hadn't sent her, or else why would she go to such lengths to stifle her screams.

"Oh, Señor. . ." she said moments later, relaxing her arms and legs. I withdrew from her and settled down next to her.

"Sparks," I said.

"Si," she whispered.

"But that's not the only reason you came here tonight, is it, little Lita?"

"Señor?"

"And don't call me señor," I told her. "My name is Clint—and don't say 'Cleent.' Your English is at least as good as your father's."

"As you wish, Clint," she said. "I would like you to work for my father. I fear that if you do not, he will surely lose to Señor Kennedy."

"Lose what? What are they fighting over?"

"Señor Kennedy lost some stock one night, many

months ago. He swore that it was my father who took them. A few days later, my father lost some stock, and he swore that it was Señor Kennedy. Since then they have been fighting.''

"Stealing each other's stock?"

She shrugged. "Who knows any longer whose cows or horses are whose," she said. "Perhaps some third party is stealing stock from both my father and Señor Kennedy, and knows that they will accuse each other. Cattle rustling is a profitable business, is it not?"

"It is, and that's an interesting thought. Have you approached your father with that idea?"

She laughed softly.

"I am a woman, Clint. Women can have no ideas when it comes to the business of men."

"Your father is a fool," I told her. "I've known a lot of women who have had worthwhile ideas in the past."

"And you've listened to them?" she asked.

"I have."

"Would you listen to me if I told you I had an idea right now?" she asked, moving her hand beneath the sheets.

I smiled at her and said, "I'm all ears."

She pressed her body against mine and said, "That is not the truth, Clint. Not at all."

9

The next morning I thanked both Victor and Lita Martinez for their hospitality—separately, of course.

"I hope that you will not give me cause to regret extending to you my hospitality, Señor Adams," Martinez told me.

"I don't have any intention of making you sorry, Señor Martinez. I'll be moving on soon, probably tomorrow. I have no intentions of getting involved in your war with Kennedy."

"Gracias, Señor. I will take your word for that."

"I hope you will make your men understand, as well," I said, remembering how the Kennedy men had tried to take me on.

"Have no fear, Señor. Esteban is my foreman. He will see to it that none of the men try to harm you. It would be an act of loyalty, but an unfortunate one."

"I agree."

"You are sure you will not work for me, Señor?" he asked.

I mounted Duke and said, "I'm positive. I'm sorry."

"Do not be sorry, Señor. If you will not work for me, I am grateful that you will not work against me. Please, if you are ever near here again, you are welcome in my house."

"I hope you settle your problems with Kennedy, Señor Martinez," I told him. I looked at the house and saw Lita watching from the window. I smiled at her, waved to her father, and headed back to the border.

I had made up my mind to pull out that night. It was the best thing for me to do. I didn't belong here, had never had any intentions of stopping here. Aside from my encounters with both Laura and Lita, I was sorry I had ever come to Lansdale.

I intended to remedy that as soon as I got back to my hotel. If I could say goodbye to Laura without too much trouble or effort, I would. Otherwise I would simply leave.

When I crossed the river into Texas I turned and stared back at the Mexican soil. The last time I had been in Mexico had been a little over a year before. I had exorcised some ghosts. Because of that I had never intended to go back.

I wheeled Duke around and headed for Lansdale. I never heard the shot, but I felt the impact as the bullet hit me high in the back, on the left side. Duke's instincts were good. He knew I was hurt and he took off running, which caused the next two shots to miss me. I leaned over and wrapped my hands around his massive neck, holding on for dear life. I only hoped I wouldn't fall off or bleed to death before we reached town.

I don't remember too much after that. I remember the pain, and the wind, but everything else was in a gray, fuzzy area. I never went totally black, just black around the edges of the gray. I didn't even realize that I was back in town until somebody's hands reached up and took me off Duke's back.

"My horse," I remember saying, "take good care of my horse."

"Don't worry," someone said, "we'll take good care of the both of you."

Maybe I knew I was safe then, because I let go then,
I let go of the edge of the black hole and fell into it. . . .

10

When I opened my eyes I was surprised, because there was no fuzziness involved. It was as if I had come immediately awake. I looked around and saw that I was in my hotel room, in bed. I tried to remember the events leading up to this, and when I moved the pain in my left shoulder brought it back. The impact of the bullet, the race with death. I had apparently outrun it—or, to be more precise, Duke had. The big fella had saved my life again, and I'd lost count of how many times he'd done that.

The door opened and a man walked in.

"Ah, you're awake," he said. He was a young man, in his early thirties, and from the black bag he was carrying I judged he was the doc who had patched me up.

"How am I, Doc?" I asked.

"Stiles is my name, Mr. Adams, and you're doing nicely, thanks to my handiwork."

"You're modest."

"I know my limitations. Your wound was not that bad. The loss of blood was more dangerous, but you got back here in plenty of time. Where were you shot?"

"By the river."

"That far away?" he asked, approaching the bed. "That horse of yours must run like the wind. Let me check your bandage while I'm here, and then I'll go for the sheriff. He wanted to know when you were awake."

"Fine."

He turned me over and probed my wound, causing me some pain.

"Good, it's still closed. It'll stay that way as long as you don't move around too much."

"How long have I been here?"

"Two days."

"My horse?"

"Yes, they told me you were concerned about him. He's in good hands at the livery."

He was clean shaven, so clean in fact that I didn't think he would be capable of growing a beard even if he wanted to. He might even have been younger than I first thought. He had a long nose and a chin to match.

"You're okay," he said, patching me back up again. "I'll go and get the sheriff."

"And a bottle," I said.

He looked at me for a moment, closing his bag, and then said, "All right, and a bottle." He started to leave and then stopped and turned to me again. "There's someone else who wanted to know when you were awake."

"Who?"

"Laura Kennedy. Shall I tell her?"

"Sure, why not. When I'm flat on my back I get kind of lonely," I said.

"I'm sure. I'll see you soon."

He left, and I did some thinking. Somebody didn't believe I was leaving town, and put a hole in me. By doing that, he made sure I wouldn't leave. It was a personal matter, now, and I wasn't leaving until it was resolved.

Oh, I still wasn't taking sides, but I'd straddle the fence awhile and see what I could come up with.

In spite of the pain in my shoulder, I felt pretty good right about then. I knew where I was going, now.

When the door opened again the sheriff came walking in. I was struck again at how small he looked, and wondered just how much trouble it had caused him in the past before he'd been able to get a handle on it.

"How do you feel, Adams?"

"Pretty good, Sheriff, I'm feeling pretty good. Should be on my feet pretty soon."

"Want to tell me what happened?" he asked.

"Sure, pull up a chair."

He did just that, and sat by the bed while I related everything to him. I told him how both Kennedy and Martinez thought I might be working for the other, and then how they both tried to hire me I told him about spending the night in Mexico, and then catching a bullet as I crossed back into Texas.

"And here I am."

"You're serious, aren't you?" he asked.

"About what?"

"About not working for either man. About your coming to town being the result of an accidental meeting between you and Laura Kennedy?"

"I'm serious, Sheriff."

"I guess you'll be leaving town as soon as you're able, then," he said.

"Actually, if I hadn't gotten shot, I'd have been gone days ago. Now I guess you're right. I'll leave when I'm able."

He took that to mean when I was physically able. As far as I was concerned, I wouldn't be leaving until I found out who shot me, and took care of him.

"You didn't see anyone?"

"Not a glance, Sheriff. I caught a bullet and my horse took off."

"A good animal. Came charging down the main street

like his tail was on fire. Took four of us to stop him and calm him down so we could get you off."

"You pulled me off?"

He smiled and said, "I had some help."

"I'm much obliged."

"Don't mention it." He stood up and looked down at me. "Adams, it would be a bad idea for you to stick around any longer than you have to. Why give whoever it was another chance at you?"

"That's one way of looking at it," I said.

"That's the only way to look at it," he said. "I wouldn't want to think you were going to go out on your own and try and find out who shot you."

"Are you going to find out?"

"I'll ask around, but you haven't given me much to go on," he explained.

"That's what I thought," I told him.

"Take my advice. As soon as you're able, leave Lansdale. I don't want the Gunsmith getting killed in my town."

I smiled at him and said, "That would put it on the map, wouldn't it?"

"I'll be seeing you," he said, and left.

Yes, sir, I thought, my getting killed in Lansdale, Texas would sure make it hard for Enoch Kennedy to keep his town all to himself. On that amusing thought, I fell asleep again.

11

When I woke up again, Laura Kennedy was in the chair by my bed.

"My gun," I said, which might have been disappointing first words for her to hear, but I needed to know where my gun was.

"On the bedpost behind you," she said. "How do you feel?" she asked.

I moved my shoulders a bit, and then said, "Okay, I guess. I'll be on my back for a while, which means I'll be stuck here in town for longer than I intended."

"And how long was that?"

"I was going to leave the morning after I got shot—if I hadn't gotten shot, that is."

"Did you see who shot you?" She seemed anxious.

"Don't you mean, did I see any of your father's men?" I didn't give her a chance to answer. "The answer is no, I didn't see any of your father's men, I didn't see any of Martinez's men, I didn't see anybody."

"I'm glad you're all right."

"I'm glad, too," I replied. "How does your father feel about it?"

"What do you mean?"

I stared at her.

"Clint, you don't think my father had anything to do with it," she said.

"Maybe I didn't convince him that I wasn't taking sides," I told her.

"That's ridiculous."

"Well, then maybe one of his men thought he'd be doing your father a favor."

"My father talked with the men you had the problem with and told them to stay away from you."

"There are a lot of other men on your father's ranch, Laura," I reminded her.

"My father talked with the foreman, and told him to keep the men in line for as long as you were in town."

"Would that be Vern?"

"No," she said. "Will you be leaving when you get back on your feet?"

"No, I don't think so."

"The sheriff said you were shot by the river," she said. "What were you doing there? Did you get lost all night?"

"No, I was coming from Victor Martinez's house. I spent the night as his guest."

"What? I thought you didn't know Martinez?"

"I didn't. Five of his men picked me up and, eh, escorted me to his house after I left your ranch."

"What did he want?"

"The same thing your father wanted. To make sure I wouldn't work for your father by hiring me away from him, or just plain hiring me."

"What did he offer you?" she asked.

"Money," I said, "and his daughter."

"His daughter?" she asked, incredulously. "That greasy little—Did you accept?"

"I did not," I said.

"But you spent the night."

"It was too dark to start back. I might have gotten

lost. He extended the hospitality of his home to me, and I accepted."

"I'll bet. Did his daughter extend her hospitality, too?"

"What do you mean?"

"Oh, never mind. What are you going to do when you recover?" she asked. "It must have been Martinez's men who shot you, so you can come to work for my father."

"I'm not coming to work for anyone, Laura. I'm going to work for myself."

"What—"

"I'm going to find out who shot me and turn him over to the sheriff."

She stared at me for a moment, trying to decide what that meant to her and her father.

"I'm not going to get in your father's way, Laura. That is, unless I find out that he had me shot."

"I told you—"

"I know what you told me, Laura, but are you so sure that your father had nothing to do with it?" I asked her. "You think about it."

She started to speak, then stopped and seemed to be thinking over what I said.

"All right," she said, finally. "We'll talk again. Get some rest, okay?"

"Okay. Thanks for coming," I said as she got up and headed for the door.

She stopped at the door, turned her head and said, "Sure."

When she was gone I wondered if I would be able to persuade her to help me. She seemed to have mixed feelings about her father. She was loyal to him, but she was also loyal to the memory of her mother, and did not agree with the method her father had chosen to honor her memory. She might just be undecided enough to help me.

12

Five days after I was shot I was back on my feet again —against doctor's orders.

"I won't be responsible—" the doctor started to say when he came into my room and found me up and dressed.

"I'm not asking you to be, Doc," I told him. "I'm grateful for what you've done. What do I owe you?"

"By bill has been taken care of."

"By who?"

"Laura Kennedy."

My first instinct was to tell him that I could pay my own bills, but I changed my mind. Let Laura have her way this time. It might make it easier to get her to help me later.

"I'll have to remember to thank her," I said, strapping on my gun.

"I'm sure," he said. "Well, I guess you don't need me anymore. If you have any discomfort it's going to be your own fault, but come and see me anyway."

"Thanks, Doc."

It was nice to be out on the street again. Five days on your back is long enough for anyone. I walked down to the sheriff's office and found him in.

"Back on your feet again, eh?" he asked. "A little early, isn't it?"

"I should be all right as long as I don't try to do any running—or riding."

"You're trying to tell me that you'll be in town a little longer," he said.

"And trying to stay out of trouble," I assured him.

"That's good," he said. He opened his desk drawer and came out with a bottle of whisky—good whisky, not saloon rotgut.

"Drink?" he asked.

"Why not?"

I sat down and took the glass he offered me. The bottle of whisky he had was the same stuff that had been in the decanters at Kennedy's house. I hadn't tasted it then, but I'd been convinced that it was the best. I tasted it now, and found out I was a good judge of whisky.

"This is good," I told him.

"It was a gift. I don't drink it too often. I don't want to get used to it."

"I know what you mean."

He was about the same size as Kennedy, only he had more meat on his bones. I had been wondering if Kennedy owned him, but now I was wondering something else. Could they be related?

"Have you made any progress trying to find out who shot me?" I asked him.

"I've checked the hands at the Kennedy ranch, and they all have alibis."

"Sure. They all alibi each other, right?"

"Somebody was always with somebody else," he told me.

"Who's the foreman out there, Sheriff? I thought maybe it was Vern whatsisname."

"He's not foreman material. He's just got a big mouth and a hot head." Then he frowned at me and asked,

"Why do you want to know?"

"I thought maybe I'd have a talk with him."

"About what?"

"Maybe about what it's like to work for a wealthy, powerful man like Enoch Kennedy."

"I don't buy that, Adams," he said, putting away his bottle of good whisky. "Look," he said, leaning his elbows on the desk and looking straight at me, "if you're going to nose around, try and do it without killing anyone."

"Sheriff, I didn't think you were the type to judge a man by his reputation. I don't usually solve my problems by killing people. Believe it or not, it's not my style."

I put down my empty glass and got up to leave.

"Stay within the law, then," he said. "I'd appreciate not having to come after you."

"But if Kennedy told you to, you would?"

He bristled and stood up to his full five and a half feet.

"Don't let my size fool you, Adams. I don't fit into anybody's pocket!"

"I guess that's something I'll have to find out for myself, Sheriff—while staying within the law, I mean."

I left, confident—for the time being, at least—that as long as I did stay within the confines of the law, I wouldn't have to deal with Sheriff Amos Cross, who—in spite of his size—I would not look forward to going up against.

13

When I told Sheriff Cross that I'd be all right as long as I didn't try to do any riding, I meant serious riding. I also told him that so that he wouldn't expect me to leave town in the near future. Even bouncing up and down on the seat of my wagon could reopen my wound.

I could have ridden out to the Kennedy ranch to talk to the foreman—whose name I still hadn't gotten—but it would have taken twice as long to get there because I wouldn't be able to let Duke run. Aside from that, I didn't expect Kennedy would welcome me with open arms. Maybe I could persuade Laura to get the two of us together.

After five days on my back, I wanted to experience the simple pleasure of walking into a saloon and ordering a beer. Even a short stretch of poker would have been nice.

I went over to the saloon where I'd had the run in with the Kennedy ranch men. Not that I hoped to run into them again—although it would have been a nice test of Enoch Kennedy's control over them—but I'd been there before, and that gave it an advantage over the other two saloons in town. At least I could call the bartender by his first name.

"Hey," Bill Chambers called as I walked in, "it's nice

to see you back on your feet."

"Thanks, Bill. How about a beer?" I said, bellying up to the bar.

"On the house," he said.

"Thanks, Bill."

I looked around the room and didn't see any of the four Kennedy men, Vern and his three friends.

When Bill brought the beer I asked him, "Are there any Kennedy men in the place, Bill?"

He took a moment to look and then said, "None that I know, Clint." He leaned forward and asked, "Was it a Kennedy man who shot you?"

I drank some beer and shook my head.

"I don't know, Bill, I didn't see anybody."

"That was some sight, Clint, that big black horse of yours carrying you down the street."

"He's something, all right," I agreed. "If it wasn't for him, I'd be dead five or six times over by now."

"I guess it's important to have a good animal when you're always on the go."

"A good animal is the most important thing," I said.

"And a good gun?"

"Unfortunately."

I turned and looked around the room again. I saw a four-handed poker game in progress and asked Bill, "Who's at the poker table?"

He looked over and said, "A couple of regulars, from town, and two men I never saw before."

"Are they together?" I asked. "The two men you don't know?"

"They didn't come in together," he told me.

"That doesn't necessarily mean anything," I said. I took my beer and walked to the table. There was a fifth chair open.

"Mind if I sit in?" I asked.

Each man signaled his agreement, and I sat down.

I was playing for only ten minutes when I realized the two strangers certainly knew each other. They were sitting with a man between them, and when I sat down I sat next to the dealer. I call him the dealer because almost every time he dealt, the other man won. He was dropping hands consistently but never for very much money. On the other hand, when the other man won, the dealer built the pots up for him. The other man was more than making up for the money the dealer was losing.

I waited until I was the sucker, until I was the one with a good enough hand to win nine times out of ten. He dealt me three of a kind on the first three cards of seven-card stud. I knew before the hand was out he'd fill me in. My three of a kind were jacks, high enough to make any man feel powerful. His partner, however, had a pair of queens on the table, and I knew he had another pair in the hole. He'd fill his friend in with a third queen on the last card, and it wouldn't come from the top of the deck.

At least, he didn't intend for his friend to get the top card.

He kept betting into me so I'd raise, and so that his friend could raise me. Then he would raise his friend, and I would raise them both again. His friend would call until he got his third queen, then I would have to stop the raising.

Only I had no intentions of stopping.

"Last card," the dealer said. I was already filled in, so it was his friend's turn now.

I reached out and clamped my hand down on the wrist of the hand that was holding the deck. His eyes went to mine and he said, "Hey!"

He was a heavy man, with big, broad hands that you would never expect could handle a deck of cards the way he was handling them. The other man was taller, slimmer, but about the same age, late thirties or thereabouts. The heavy man wore a Navy Colt on his hip, but the taller man appeared unarmed. He'd have a hideaway gun somewhere on him, though.

"What's the idea?" the dealer asked.

"Put the deck down on the table," I told him.

"What for? I don't deal that way."

"Put it down, friend. I want to make sure we all get our cards from the top of the deck."

He bristled and said, "Are you accusing me of cheating? You better be able to prove it, friend."

"I'll prove it," I told him, eying him coldly. "Deal the last card, friend."

He put the deck down and, eying his cohort nervously, he dealt the last card to the players still in the game —himself, me, and his partner.

"You been betting dealer," I told him. He had a pair of kings on the table and nothing else, I was sure. The kings gave him the lead bet, however.

He bet ten dollars and I said, "Betting right into two raisers again, eh?" I asked. "You've either got a good hand, or a bad head for cards, friend," I told him. "I raise twenty."

The other man played it straight, as if he had no idea what was going on. He peered at his last card and hid his surprise well. He called my raise. I think he was probably afraid to go out.

"Now you, friend," I told the dealer. "You've been betting like crazy. Go ahead, call my raise."

The dealer eyed me warily, and threw the twenty dollars in.

I turned over my hand, revealing jacks-full.

"Let's see yours," I told the dealer's partner. The other two men were watching closely.

The man turned over his cards, revealing two pair, queens and fours.

"And you," I told the dealer.

He turned his over, revealing that he had nothing in the hole. He was holding only kings.

"You men should watch who you play with," I told the other two men.

"How does this prove I was cheating?" the dealer asked.

"We'd be interested in that too, Mister," one of the other men said.

"These two are working together," I told them. "Almost every time tubby here had the deal, his friend won the hand. Think about it."

"Not this time, though," the man across from me said.

"That's because I made him deal from the table," I told him.

I reached for the deck and flipped it over, revealing the bottom card. It was a queen.

"This was supposed to be his friend's last card, filling him in. He filled me in a long time ago."

Both men turned their eyes on the heavy dealer, who tried to talk his way out of it.

"He's crazy. That's just a coincidence," he said, pointing to the queen.

"Then tell us why you bet into two raisers, and even raised back, with only a pair of kings, if you weren't building a pot for your friend," I said.

That was when his friend went for his hideaway. I picked up the deck and flipped the cards into his face. With my left foot, I flipped his chair over backwards. The other man started to go for his gun, but I shouted, "Don't!"

He froze, but he was still a second away from continuing the move.

"Friend, I don't want to kill you over a few dollars," I said. "But if you go for that gun, I will. That goes for your friend, too."

I don't know what they would have done if the other

two men at the table hadn't produced their guns and covered the two cheaters.

"Pick up your friend and get out," I told the dealer. "Be grateful that these men don't take you out and hang you."

The dealer's eyes went wide when he heard the word "hang," and he pushed his chair back.

"Move carefully, friend," I told him.

He circled the table carefully and helped his chum to his feet. The taller man's hideaway was on the floor, but they ignored it and stumbled over each other getting to the door.

"We're much obliged, Mister," one of the men said as both put their guns away.

"Take what you lost," I told them.

"You take the pot, Mister. You earned it. We'll split what they left on the table."

"Fair enough," I said, and raked in my pot. I had come out a few hundred dollars ahead, and that was all right. I'd only sat down to pass the time, anyway.

I went to the bar and told Bill to get me another beer.

"On the house, again," he said.

I dropped some coins on the bar and told him, "On the two who just left."

I spent much of the afternoon in the saloon, talking with Bill, who had come to Lansdale about five or six years before and gotten his job tending bar.

"Have you ever met Enoch Kennedy?" I asked.

"Nope. I've seen him, but he never comes in here. He's goes into the saloon down the street," he said. "The one that he owns."

"That figures."

"That scrawny old bastard commands a lot of respect around here, Clint," he told me.

"I know it. Tell me something."

"What?"

"Amos Cross, how long has he been sheriff?"

"Couple of years."

"How did he get the job?"

He looked down and said, "He won the election."

"But. . ."

"Nobody I spoke to voted for him."

"You mean the election was rigged?"

"Who knows for sure?"

"I'll bet Enoch Kennedy knows."

He nodded.

"Bill, do you know the name of Kennedy's foreman?"

"That'd be Deke Bronson," he told me. "If you're planning on tangling with him, Clint, be careful. He's a bad one. He especially hates Mexicans, but he's a bad one no matter who you are."

"Deke Bronson," I said. I finished my beer and told him, "I'll remember what you said, Bill. Thanks."

"Anytime."

I left the saloon and headed back to my hotel. It was my first day out, and I was feeling it. I wanted to get back to my room and rest up.

When I entered my room somebody was in my bed, asleep. I was annoyed with myself because I had entered so carelessly.

I closed the door behind me and walked to the bed to wake Laura Kennedy. When I touched her shoulder she rolled over and looked up at me, but not with Laura Kennedy's eyes.

It was Lita Martinez.

14

"Lita!"

She pouted and said, "You are not happy to see me?"

"I'm just surprised. How did you get here? Why did you come?"

She gave me a coy look and flattened her arms at her sides, pressing the sheet tightly against her body. She was naked underneath and the sheet molded itself to her curves.

"First get into bed with me, and I will tell you," she said.

"Come on, Lita, I'm in no mood."

"No mood?" she asked, and then she lowered the sheet to her waist and added, "For this?"

Her breasts were perfect mounds of flesh, topped by large, brown nipples that were blossoming while I watched.

I took the sheet from her waist and brought it back up to her neck.

"Talk first," I told her. "Did anyone see you come up here?"

"I came up the back."

"This was foolish," I said. "This is Kennedy's town, if anyone saw you—"

"You are worried for me. How sweet."

"I'm worried for me, too. This could make someone believe that I'm working for your father. You could get me killed, Lita."

"But that is why I'm here," she said.

"What?"

"My father sent me, Clint," she said. "We heard that you were wounded."

"Heard? How?"

"We have ears," she said. "My father sent me to tell you that you were not shot by his men. This he swears."

"He risked sending you to tell me that, his own daughter?" I asked.

"He wanted you to believe it," she said, simply.

And I did, but I had also believed Laura. If Kennedy hadn't ordered me shot, and Martinez hadn't, then who had?

Lita's remark about a third party being involved came to mind again. It was something well worth looking into.

"Now that we've talked," Lita said, lowering the sheet again, "will you get into bed?"

I began unbuttoning my shirt. "You'll have to be gentle with me, little Lita. I'm a wounded man."

"I will do everything, Clint," she assured me, "everything for your pleasure, and mine."

She helped me undress and then I lay down on my back. She was true to her word. She did just about everything a woman could possibly do to a man, using her hands, her mouth, her *hair*. Several times I didn't think I'd be able to bear it, but she went on and on until finally she mounted me and guided me into her warm, slick tunnel.

She began to ride up and down, and I had been in this position before. Again I was reminded of my previous trip to Mexico, where I had been wounded and in this position with two other women. Soon, though, I wasn't able to think of anything but the insistent pressure she was inflicting on me with her muscles, and finally I reached the point where I couldn't take it any longer and I let go inside of her.

"Rest," she said, "you need rest."

"If I didn't before," I said, "I do now."

15

Five more days of inactivity and I was starting to get mighty itchy. During that additional five days I did nothing more strenuous than play poker and hoist beer mugs. During those five days, no one from the Kennedy spread showed his face in town, and that was a disappointment. I had been hoping that since I couldn't go to them, they'd come to me.

An even bigger disappointment was that, during that time, Laura never came to town, either. There was more than one reason why that was disappointing.

Then there was the fact that every time I turned around it seemed I ended up looking right into Amos Cross's eyes. Not that I blamed him, he was just doing his job, keeping his eye on potential trouble.

The morning of the eleventh day I decided it was time to test the shoulder. Duke needed the exercise too. I didn't want Sheriff Cross on my tail during the ride, so I used the back door of the hotel and went right over to the livery.

"He's been getting mighty itchy, Mr. Adams," Jed told me.

"That makes two of us, Jed. Saddle him up for me, will you?"

"Sure. Glad to see you feeling better."

"Yeah, me too."

When Jed brought Duke out for me the big fella seemed raring to go. He rolled his eyes and flared his nostrils at me, and I patted his neck to calm him down.

"Easy, big boy. We don't want you using up all your energy before we get going. I patted him hard. "Let's see if I can get into the saddle without falling off."

I took him out of town at a light trot. There was some discomfort in my shoulder, but it wasn't really as bad as I might have expected.

I never got Duke up to full speed, but I gave him enough of his head for him to stretch out the kinks. Once we were well clear of town, and I knew I wasn't being followed, I turned him towards the Rio Grande. I wanted to go back to the spot where I'd been shot and look around. I had no doubt that Amos Cross was a good man in his own way, but I didn't think he had ridden all the way out here after the incident. The fact that I couldn't identify anyone pretty much closed the matter, as far as he was concerned.

As far as I was concerned the matter was still very much open, and it was going to stay that way until I closed it.

After that night with Lita Martinez, I had sent her back to her father with the assurance that I believed he had nothing to do with my getting shot. It was only a small lie. Wanting to believe it was close to believing it. All I needed was some additional evidence to convince me of his, and Kennedy's, innocence. Evidence, and the guy who was guilty.

After a couple of false stops I finally arrived at what I thought was the spot. Duke tossed his head a couple of times and looked around warily, and I knew I had found it.

"Don't get nervous," I told Duke, dismounting. I looked around, trying to decide where the shots might have come from. When I thought I had it figured I mounted up again and walked Duke over to a spot about twenty yards away, on the Texas side of the river, behind a spray of rocks large enough for a man to hide behind.

I dismounted again and took a look behind the rocks. I got lucky. Whoever it had been had not picked up his spent cartridges. Perhaps he'd tried to catch me and had left in a hurry. I picked up the cartridges for a closer look and found that they were .44 caliber. That didn't really tell me a lot. Too many rifles and revolvers fired .44 caliber rounds for the information to be of great help. Hell, my guns fired .44's. I dropped the shell casings into my vest pocket anyway, though, just in case I needed them later.

There were some bootprints in the dirt, indicating a large foot. That eliminated Amos Cross and Enoch Kennedy—as well as Laura Kennedy and Lita Martinez. With four down, though, there were still plenty of suspects.

I had found out all I could and mounted up again.

"Let's go back to town, Duke," I said. What I really wanted to do was ride out to the Kennedy ranch, but if Enoch Kennedy didn't want me there, there was a chance I'd have to explain my actions to Sheriff Cross— from the wrong side of a cell. I wanted to avoid a confrontation with Cross for as long as I could.

I wouldn't be able to accomplish anything if I was behind bars. For that reason, it wasn't so much Cross I was looking to avoid, but the *law*.

I had to be careful with Cross, because I still didn't know if he was in Kennedy's pocket. Still, I wanted to get back to town and dump a couple of those spent shells in his lap, to see how he'd react. I'd keep one for myself, kind of like an ace in the hole.

I wanted to hear him explain why he hadn't found them himself.

16

I dropped two of the spent shells in his hand, and he stared at them for a moment. Then he raised his eyes to mine and said, "So?"

"You never rode out there, did you?" I tried my best to keep any hint of an accusation out of my tone.

"As a matter of fact, Mr. Adams, I did not," Cross said, dropping the shells on the desk.

"Why not?"

"I don't think you need the answer to that, Adams, but I'll give it to you," he said, leaning forward. "Call it professional courtesy for an ex-lawman—but don't count on it happening again. Okay?"

"Sure."

"You can't identify the man who shot you, so these casings are no good. There are too many .44 caliber weapons in town. I can't accuse every man who carries that caliber," he said, eying my holster.

"Yeah," I answered. "Okay."

"Did my answer satisfy you?" he asked.

"What do you mean?"

"You're wondering if I'm in Enoch Kennedy's employ, aren't you?" he asked.

"Are you?"

"Professional courtesy just went out the door," he

told me, suddenly. Pointing he said, "That door. I'd appreciate it if you'd go out the same way. Doc says you're not ready for heavy traveling yet, so I'm not booting you out of town. Kicking you out of my office is the next best thing."

I showed him the palms of both of my hands and said, "I'm going, Sheriff, I'm going." When I reached for the shells on his desk he covered them with his hand.

"I'll hold on to these."

"Whatever you say, Sheriff."

I started for the door and he called my name.

"Adams!"

"Yeah."

"Whether I'm working for Enoch Kennedy or not, he's a prominent man in this town—hell, he is *the* prominent man in town. I won't have him harassed. Understood?"

"Perfectly, Sheriff," I said, and left.

His actions and reactions had told me next to nothing. Either way, he could have acted the same way. He was smart, though, I had no doubt about that. I only hoped that, if and when the time came, he would be smart enough to back me up.

17

I was tired from the ride to the border, but I was also hungry and thirsty. Otherwise I felt fine, and the exercise had probably done me good.

I went over to the saloon and asked Bill if he could get me something to eat.

"If you're not choosy," he said.

"Whatever you've got is fine," I assured him.

"Beer while you wait?" he asked.

"You read my mind."

I took the beer to a corner table and sat with my back to the wall. It felt good to relax and stretch my legs under the table. I hadn't realized how tired I really was until Bill nudged me and put a plate down in front of me.

"You looked like you dozed off, Clint," he said. "Are you all right?"

"Yes, I'm fine," I told him, rubbing my eyes. "I guess I overtaxed myself, this morning. Thanks, Bill."

"Sure."

The meal was a simple dish, meat and potatoes, but it did the trick. After a pot of strong coffee, I felt better as far as hunger and thirst were concerned, but I was still feeling fatigue.

"Thanks, Bill. I'm going over to the hotel. See you later."

"Sure thing, Clint."

My instincts and the desk clerk told me that Laura Kennedy was in my room. She was seated on the bed, fully dressed. She had something other than sex on her mind and, in fact, so did I.

"Hello," I said, shutting the door. "The clerk told me you were up here."

"I told him, too," she said. "I didn't want to get shot."

"Where have you been?" I asked.

"At the ranch. My father doesn't want me to see you, anymore," she explained.

"And you don't always do what your father wants, right?"

"I do when it suits me," she said, "but I'm a grown woman. I have a mind of my own."

"I've noticed that. Are you here for any special reason?"

"Yes, I am," she said, and then fell silent. She had something on her mind, but wasn't sure she wanted to voice it.

"Whenever you're ready," I said, "you can tell me about it, but if you wait too long, you're going to have to wake me to do it."

I walked around to the other side of the bed and lay down next to her on my back. She turned around and looked at me over my shoulder.

"Are you all right?"

"Yes, I'm just going to take a nap."

"Now?"

"That was my plan, unless you've got something to tell me that's worth staying awake for."

"Um, yes," she said. "I want to help you."

"Help me what?"

"Find out who shot you."

"Why?"

"Because—"

"You want to know one way or the other if your father was involved," I said.

Her shoulders slumped and she said, "Yes."

I reached up and touched her face and said, "All right, Laura, and for your sake, I hope he had nothing to do with it."

"What can I do?" she asked.

"I want to talk with your father's foreman, Deke Bronson."

She shuddered. "Deke's mean, Clint. I don't know if he'd want to *just* talk to you."

"Can you get him to meet me?" I asked.

"Yes," she said, without hesitation.

"Just like that?"

"He . . . likes me. If I ask him to meet you, he will. I don't know what he'll do once he does, though."

"Let me worry about that."

"What about your shoulder?" she asked.

"Let me worry about that," I said again.

She leaned over me and kissed me, probing with her tongue.

"Can I stay here with you for a little while?" she asked.

I reached out and took her by the back of the neck with my right hand.

"Why not?"

"Um," she said, kissing me again. "What about your nap?"

I pulled her down to me and said, "Let me worry about that."

18

After Laura left I slept like a baby. The extra exertion she supplied was just enough to send me off the moment she shut the door behind her.

I woke up in time for dinner and poker. I had eaten the former and was thoroughly engrossed in the latter when some familiar faces entered the saloon.

Vern and Fred came in with two other men I didn't know. Vern spotted me right off and said something to Fred. I pressed my back more firmly against the wall and drew one card to an inside straight. I was feeling lucky. Turned out I was lucky enough to fill in, but lose to a flush. There are all different kinds of luck. Sometimes you can get just what you want, but it isn't enough.

I wanted Deke Bronson. I wondered if he had sent these men in ahead of him.

I watched them as they went up to the bar and ordered their drinks. I divided my attention between them and the next hand and lost on a miscalculation. I hoped that if they had something to say or do, they'd say it or do it before I went broke.

They stayed at the bar for half an hour, drinking and laughing. After the first ten minutes I started paying more attention to my cards than to them, and I was winning again.

Forty minutes after they came in, they threw some money on the bar and left without looking over at me.

As I expected, Bill came over to me almost immediately and said, "The Kennedy spread boys left this for you, Clint." He handed me a folded piece of paper.

I slipped it into my vest pocket. I'd read it back at my hotel room. If Bronson thought I was going to meet him at night, he was stupid, and if he was Kennedy's choice for foreman, I doubted that was true. More than likely the note would either name place and time for the following day, or would tell me to go to hell.

Either way, I wasn't going to let it influence my poker game. My luck was too good.

It hadn't taken Laura very long to convince Bronson he should at least send me an answer. I wondered just how much he liked her, and how close they might be. She was certainly no virgin, and I wouldn't hold it against her if she was friendly with him. Especially if it turned out that it had done me some good.

I played for another hour, and when the luck started to go bad I bid the other players good night, waved to Bill, and went back to my room with a bottle.

In my room I settled down on the bed with the open bottle, and fished the note out of my pocket.

It was short and to the point: "You want to talk, meet me two miles South of town, in the arroyo, one hour after sunup. Only chance." It was signed: "D.B."

An hour after the sun came up. That probably meant he'd be there before the sun came up.

I settled down to get a good night's sleep, because I intended to be there an hour *before* the sun came up.

I wondered if he'd come alone.

Even if he didn't, I wondered who the hell I could have possibly brought with *me*, anyway.

19

When you think you're one step ahead of somebody, don't just look behind. You might find yourself bumping into something—like the lip of a grave.

I rode out to that arroyo, two miles south of town, but I rode east and came up to the arroyo from that point. The Kennedy spread was west of town, and Bronson would have to come from that direction to reach the arroyo—under normal conditions, that is. If he was really there just to talk, that's what he should do. Then again, all I wanted was to talk, and look what I was doing.

I left Duke within easy walking distance of the meeting point, and continued on foot. I walked along the wide arroyo, coming from the east, and up ahead I could see a dark figure walking towards me, coming from the west.

Two minds with the same idea.

"Bronson," I called out.

"Is that you, Adams?" a voice answered. "You're early, aren't you?"

"So are you."

"I guess we both had the same idea."

"I don't know," I answered, "what was yours?"

"Just to talk."

"Then I guess we've got the same idea," I told him. "Come ahead and we'll talk."

There was hesitation, and then he said, "I can hear you fine, Adams. What's on your mind."

I sat down on a large rock, wondering if he didn't have some men out there trying to aim at my voice. "I want to know whether your boss ordered me shot ten days ago."

"My orders are to stay away from you, Adams. You might be working for Martinez, and then again you might not."

"What do you think, Bronson?"

"I think we'd be better off with you dead, Adams, but that's not my decision to make."

"And your men?"

"They're loyal to Mr. Kennedy. I wouldn't be surprised if that bullet in your shoulder was a Mexican bullet, Adams. Have you checked into that?"

"I have. They say they didn't do it, either."

"You can't believe a Mex. They're all lying savages."

It was starting to get lighter, but I still couldn't make out any more than a shadowy figure. We were a good twenty-five feet apart, shouting at each other in the dark. I would have liked to see what he looked like, but he seemed in a hurry to get going.

"Is that all, Adams? I've got work to do, you know."

"Why don't we sit down somewhere and discuss this, Bronson," I suggested.

"I like it fine this way, Adams. Hell, this way I can tell my boss I didn't see you, and I won't be lying, will I?"

That was one way of looking at it.

"I'm leaving, Adams. I don't expect to hear from you again, or see you—that is, unless Mr. Kennedy suddenly decides you should die. Then I'll come looking for you."

I started to back away, not wanting to stand up straight and present a better target, just in case he had a couple of men with rifles planted somewhere.

"Adams," he called out again. "I'm leaving, Adams."

Might as well make him think I was long gone, which I was suddenly wishing I was. It was getting lighter by the minute, and pretty soon I'd be a target no decent rifleman could miss.

I thought I heard someone mutter, "Shit," and I hoped it was Bronson. Maybe he did have me set up, and now he thought he'd blown it.

"Adams," he called again. He was too eager for me to speak up again, probably so that his men could locate their target.

I came to a spray of large rocks and dropped to my belly. A horse moved away from me. Instead of standing up, I waited, still listening.

After a good ten minutes it was dusk. If I moved I'd be in plain sight, so I stayed where I was. Suddenly, I heard what sounded like a boot scattering rocks.

"Watch your step," someone whispered.

"How the hell long do we have to stay out here, anyway?" another voice demanded.

"Until we make sure that he ain't out here somewhere. We didn't hear no horse, did we?"

"So, maybe he left his horse so far away we wouldn't have heard it anyway. Come on, Fred, let's go back."

Fred. There was a name I knew. The other man didn't sound like Vern, but now that I had a name, I recognized Fred's voice.

I listened intently as they walked the arroyo, coming towards me. I couldn't afford to be found lying on my belly, so I picked up a fist-sized rock and threw it as far as I could to the north.

"What was that?" one voice asked, and I stood up as quickly as I could, ignoring the discomfort in my shoulder.

The two of them were no more than ten feet from me,

looking in the direction I'd thrown the rock.

"You boys looking for me?" I asked.

They both froze, and then turned slowly. They had their rifles in their left hands, and they dropped their right hands down by their holsters.

"Before you make a move for a gun, fellas, I should tell you that I can easily kill both of you."

Fred was standing on my left, and he moistened his lips with his tongue. The other man had been one of the four who had come into the saloon the night before.

"Now, I don't want to kill either one of you. I would much rather have a nice talk, and get some information."

The man I didn't know looked at Fred, as if he would follow the other man's lead. Fred was the one to talk to, then.

"What do you say, Fred? A few answers and we can all be on our way."

Fred couldn't seem to get his lips wet enough.

"Fred," I repeated.

"I ain't telling you nothing."

"Fred," the other man said shakily.

"Shut up!" Fred snapped. "If you back me up, we can take him, Dobbs."

"Fred, that there's the Gunsmith—" the man called Dobbs started to say, but Fred cut him off viciously.

"I know who he is, goddamn it!" he snapped. "I still say we can take him. Don't let him scare you none, Dobbs. He's just a man."

"That's right, Dobbs. I'm just a man, I can bleed like anyone else. I'll tell you what, though. Why don't you let Fred make his move alone, and after I get rid of him, you can answer my questions for me. What do you say to that?"

From the look on Dobbs's face, he didn't mind that little idea at all.

Fred, on the other hand, didn't *take* to it at all.

"He's trying to separate us, Dobbs. Don't let him. If we stick together, we can take him."

"Fred, if you had two more men just like you, you still couldn't take me. Please, I'm asking you, don't make me kill you. Not over a few answers to a few questions."

"W-what kind of questions?" Dobbs asked.

"I want to know who shot me, who ordered it, and who's running the cattle across the river at night. Are Kennedy and Martinez really stealing cattle from each other, or is there some third party playing them off against each other?"

Fred's eyes widened and I knew he was going to make a move.

"Shit," he muttered and he went for his gun with a resigned look on his face, as if he knew he had no choice.

I watched his hand as it went towards his holster and I shot him before he even touched it. I had intended to shoot him in the arm, but he must have had an idea of moving as he drew, to throw me off, and he did just that. He also threw himself smack into the path of my bullet, and it caught him in the belly, knocking him onto his back.

Dobbs never moved, just watched as Fred was thrown to the ground and lay there moaning.

"What's it going to be, Dobbs?" I asked.

He looked up from Fred's squirming body, and then dropped his rifle and showed me his palms.

"I'll tell you whatever you wanna know," he said.

"That's fine," I said, holstering my gun.

I heard the shot and saw the right side of Dobbs head get blown clear off. I hit dirt and rock, banging my wounded shoulder painfully.

I rolled, and when I stopped rolling I could hear the sound of hoofbeats fading away. Whoever had fired the shot didn't want to stick around to try another. He'd accomplished his purpose.

He'd kept Dobbs from answering any questions, and I'd done the same to Fred.

My question was this: why hadn't the rifleman shot me instead of Dobbs?

20

During the ride back to town I decided to play this thing very cautious. There was a good chance right now that I might end up behind bars, and that was one thing I didn't want.

After I put Duke back up at the livery, I went looking for Bill Chambers. He was in the saloon, setting up the day's business.

"What are you doing up and around so early?" he asked me, his face reflecting his surprise.

"I need a favor, Bill."

"Well, come on in and let's talk about it," he said. I walked in and he locked the door behind us. We were alone in the place except for the swamper.

"I never thought to ask you if you owned this place." I said to him.

"I do. It's not the biggest place in town, but I save some money doing the bartending myself. Pull up a chair." He indicated a table on which sat a pot of coffee and some cups.

"What's the problem?"

I told him the story of meeting Bronson out at the arroyo, and of the two men that had been left behind to finish me. I told him that I had killed one of them, and the other had been shot by someone else, from ambush.

"Bronson left them behind," he concluded. "He set you up by agreeing to meet you."

"That's the most likely conclusion," I told him. "It's also possible that he didn't know anything about the other two men."

Bill shook his head. "From what I understand, Clint, Bronson rules that crew with an iron hand. You going to the sheriff?"

"That's why I wanted to talk to you," I said. "I don't want to go to the sheriff because I'm not sure of him. As far as I'm concerned, you're the only man in town I can trust. If Bronson or Kennedy go to the sheriff, claiming I killed their men, I want to be able to say I was with somebody."

"This morning?"

"Yeah."

"Well, you're not my type, but I think I can work something out," he said.

"I'd appreciate it."

"If the sheriff asks, tell him you were in a private poker game. He can ask me about it. I'll tell him you were there with me."

"What about the other players?"

"What other players?"

"Can you convince him?"

"I'll just tell him that the names of the players are confidential, and yours is the only one I'll mention."

"I owe you for this, Bill," I told him, finishing my coffee.

"No problem, Clint. It's my pleasure if I can help you in any way."

"What did you do before you came here, Bill?"

"I was a school teacher, back East," he said.

"You're not my idea of a school teacher."

"That's an opinion a lot of people agreed with—including me. I came West, found this town, and opened this saloon with some of my savings."

"How well do you do here?"

"I make a living, Clint, and I'm satisfied with that."

"You're a lucky man, to have a life you're satisfied with."

"I suppose so. More coffee?"

"I don't think so. I'm going back to my hotel. I want it to look as if I just finished a long, all night poker session. If the sheriff comes for me, it'll probably be early. I'll see you later and we can compare notes."

"Okay. I'll let you out."

At the door I said, "Thanks again, Bill."

"Don't mention it. See you later."

I went back to the hotel, staggering as if I'd been up all night. When I had left earlier, it had been by the back door. The day clerk was on duty, but I was sure that the sheriff would be thorough and question the night clerk as well. Whatever they said, however, I could always claim having left the hotel by the back door to attend the poker game.

When I reached my room I undressed and lay down. No sooner had my head hit the pillow than I was asleep. My last thought was that it was lucky I'd remembered to reload my gun.

21

I was awakened by an insistent banging on my door.

"Open up, Adams," a voice called. When I was fully conscious, I recognized the voice as that of Sheriff Amos Cross. The performance was about to start.

"I'm coming, hold on," I called out.

"Hurry it up, Adams," he shouted. When I opened the door he stormed in, looking me up and down, as if he expected to find me covered with blood.

"You've gone too far, Adams," he told me, looking around the room. He finally located what he was looking for and crossed over to it. My gun.

First he checked to see if it had been fired, and then he checked the loads.

"Fully loaded, but you would have taken care of that right away," he said. Then, waving my guns around, he said, "But it's been fired."

"So?" I asked. "What am I supposed to have done, Sheriff?"

"You know very well what you've done." His slight frame was stiff with rage.

"Suppose you tell me, Sheriff. Humor me."

He tucked my gun into his belt and placed his hands on his hips.

"This morning, before sun up, you went to a prear-

ranged meeting with Deke Bronson, the foreman of the
Kennedy ranch. While you were there, you killed two of
the Kennedy men, Fred Bogart and Hump Dobbs."

"How did I do that?"

"How do men like you kill, Adams?" he demanded.
"You shot them down!"

"Both of them?" I asked.

"Yes."

"With my gun?"

"With what else?"

"Have the bullets been dug out of their bodies yet,
Sheriff?" I asked.

"They will be, shortly."

"Good, then you can compare them to my gun and
find out the truth."

"Meanwhile, you'll stay in my jail."

"While I do that, why don't you go over and talk to
Bill Chambers at his saloon," I suggested.

"Chambers? Why?"

"He can tell you where I was this morning, Sheriff,
when you say I was gunning down two men."

He frowned at me. "Are you saying you never met
Bronson at the arroyo two miles south of town."

"I was playing poker all night until sun up, Sheriff.
You can ask Chambers."

"Damn it, you're still coming with me. None of your
fast talk is going to save you from spending time in my
jail."

"That's up to you, Sheriff, but you're going to feel
mighty silly about this."

"That may be," he said. "Get dressed."

While I dressed, he picked up my rifle and sniffed the
barrel, then frowned because it hadn't been fired. When
the bullets were removed from the bodies, one would be
.44 caliber, which had come from my gun. The other
came from a rifle, the caliber of which I didn't know. If

I was lucky, it would be something other than a .44, which would let my rifle out.

Dressed, I said, "I'm ready, Sheriff."

"Let's go."

He followed me out of the hotel and marched me to his jail.

It was the first time in my life I would be on the other side of the bars.

22

By mid-afternoon I figured that Cross had had enough time to prove or disprove my innocence, and was just letting me stew awhile.

Finally, after I'd spent about eight hours behind bars, Cross returned to his office.

"Hey, Sheriff," I called. "When do you serve lunch and dinner in this place?"

He frowned at me and took the keys to the cell off its wall hook. He unlocked the door to my cell and said, "You're free to go, Adams."

"Is that so?" I asked, walking out of that little room. "Did you find out your mistake?"

"There are conflicting facts that prevent me from holding you, Adams," he told me, seating himself behind his desk, "but I know damn well that you shot those men."

"What about my alibi?"

"Your story stands up, but it's just a lot of shit, and we both know it."

"What about the bullets?"

He didn't answer right away, and I knew I had him there.

"One man was killed with a forty-four," he said, "the other with a thirty-six."

"Well, well," I said, "both of my guns fire forty-fours. I guess that leaves me out, doesn't it?"

He didn't answer. He opened the bottom drawer of his desk and took out my gun.

"Here's your gun. Your rifle is over there," he said, indicating a corner of the room. "Your gunbelt is back in your room. Get out of here, Adams. You're getting away with it—this time. Don't press your luck."

"I know it's hard to admit when you're wrong, Sheriff."

"I'm not wrong," he said, banging a fist down on his desk. "I just can't prove I'm right."

"Who was the witness, Sheriff?" I asked. "There must have been a witness who said he saw me shoot those men."

"Never mind. I don't want another dead body on my hands," he told me. "Get out of here. Take my advice and get out of this town."

"Is that advice?"

"It is, for now. When I order you out of town, you'll know it."

"You're the sheriff, Sheriff," I told him, heading for the door.

"Try not to forget that, Adams," he called after me.

"I'll give it my best shot," I promised.

23

I had a taste in my throat like no other I'd ever had. After only eight hours behind bars, it was an experience I never wanted to come across again.

I went to Bill Chamber's saloon to wash the taste away with a few beers.

"How'd it go?" Bill asked.

"I was about to ask you the same thing," I told him. "Let me have a beer, will you?"

"Sure."

When he came back with it I said, "I guess he bought the story—in part, anyway. He had to cut me loose because of conflicting stories."

"You find out who turned you in?" he asked.

I shook my head. "No, but it had to be either Bronson, or Kennedy."

"And who was the third man?" he asked. "The one who killed Dobbs before you could get him to talk?"

"Somebody from the Kennedy spread," I said. "If it wasn't Bronson himself, then maybe it was Vern."

"Or Clete Smith."

"Smith?" I asked. I seemed to remember the name. "That first night—" I started to say, but he anticipated the question.

"He was with Vern and Fred, and the other man," he said.

I tried to remember, but I couldn't remember Clete Smith's face.

"I guess I better talk to Cletus Smith," I said aloud.

"The same way you talked to Bronson?" he asked.

"No. I'll take a couple of more days to make sure my shoulder's okay, and then I'll take a ride out to the Kennedy spread."

"Are you convinced it's Kennedy behind this, and not Martinez?" Bill asked.

"I'm not convinced of anything," I told him. "The Kennedy spread's closer, that's all."

"That mean you'll be riding into Mexico, too?"

"Probably. This morning makes twice that somebody tried to have me killed. I'm even more determined to find out who that somebody is."

"Well, I'll help you all I can," he said.

"Thanks, but you've already done plenty. I hope you don't get into a jam because of this poker story."

"No problem."

"Thanks for the beer," I said, throwing a coin up onto the bar.

I started for the door, but then thought of another question. "What's the closest town to the Martinez ranch?"

"That would be El Toro Rojo. At least, they buy most of their supplies and do most of their drinking there."

"El Toro Rojo," I repeated. "Can you tell me how to get there?"

"Sure," he said, and proceeded to give me directions that were easy enough to follow. The Mexican town was almost the same distance from the border as Lansdale.

After talking to Cletus Smith—and Laura Kennedy again—that would be my next stop.

24

Laura was the one who had set up the meeting with
Deke Bronson. For that reason I wanted very much to
talk to her again. I wanted to know how hard she'd had
to persuade Bronson to meet with me, if it had taken any
persuading at all.

I went over to the telegraph office. I wanted to use
Enoch Kennedy's private line to send Laura a message.

"Can I help you, Mister?" the telegraph operator
asked.

"Yes. I'd like to send a message to the Kennedy
ranch."

He was young, in his early twenties. He said, "I
couldn't do that, Mister. I'm just a relief operator.
George Bates is the only one who can operate the Kennedy line."

"When will he be back?" I asked.

" 'bout an hour, I guess."

"I'll come back."

"You can, but I don't believe it'll do you any good,"
he pointed out.

"Why is that?"

"That line is only supposed to be used for Kennedy
ranch business, by people from the Kennedy ranch."

"But Bates is the man to see."

"Yes, sir."

"I'll come back and give it a try," I said. "Thanks."

I went back to my hotel room and cleaned both of my weapons. I wanted to make sure they were in perfect working condition for what was to come. From my saddle bag I took a 57mm-long, .22-caliber Colt New Line, cleaned it, and loaded it. I'd carry that tucked into my belt, inside my shirt. I had taken it off a dead man, and it had saved my life immediately after that. I hadn't used it since.

I buttoned my shirt, strapped on my gun, and then returned to the telegraph office.

George Bates was a portly man of medium height, with gray hair and closely set, squinty eyes. "Can't do it," he said.

"Why not?"

"Can't use that line for any business other than Kennedy business."

"This is Kennedy business. I want to get a message to Laura Kennedy."

He gave me an exasperated look and said, "Mister, nobody can send messages over that private line unless he works for the Kennedy spread."

I took some money out of my pocket, and when he saw it he shook his head. "Ain't no amount of money can make me risk my job, Mister," he said. "Or my neck. Sorry."

I put my money away. "Thanks anyway."

Bates was afraid of Kennedy, that much was obvious. I wondered how many other people were afraid.

From the telegraph office I went to see the doctor, so he could check on the progress of my shoulder wound.

"You're doing fine," he said. "There's a little inflammation but nothing too serious. Did you strain yourself?"

"A little."

"That's why. No reason why you can't leave town in a few days, if that's what you want to do."

"The chances are very good that that's exactly what I'll do," I said, putting my shirt back on. "Thanks, Doc."

I decided to give Laura two more days to get in touch with me. If she didn't, I'd head for Mexico and start nosing around on that side of the border.

If she didn't get in touch with me, I might have to assume that it was because she set me up. I'd already pretty much decided that whoever was out to kill me was American, not Mexican. I'd seen no signs that anybody from Martinez's ranch was after me. I might even go to Martinez and try to recruit his help. Maybe we could find out who was trying to kill me, and who was rustling his cattle at the same time.

My prime suspects were Bronson, Cletus Smith, and Vern. Just because they were involved, that didn't mean Enoch Kennedy was. That was what I had to find out. Were they after me on their own, or under orders from him?

And where did Laura fit in? Certainly, there was no love lost between her and her father. Could she be working against him, with Bronson, rustling cattle from him and Martinez and setting the two big ranchers against each other?

Had she set me up for Bronson and his men at the arroyo? She had two days to convince me that she hadn't—if she cared to.

25

She took her sweet time.

It wasn't until the night of the second day, the night before I intended to leave for Mexico, that Laura came to my room.

When I opened the door and saw her standing there, I said, "Well, it's about time."

"Can I come in?"

"Are you alone?"

"Of course."

I stood back and let her in with my gun in my hand. I checked the hall, found it empty, and then closed the door.

"I heard about what happened when you went to meet Bronson," she said.

"Did you, now? From Bronson himself? He tell you he set me up for two of his boys?"

"I heard you killed two men."

"That's not true, Laura. I was set up, by Bronson—and maybe by you, unless you can convince me otherwise."

"Me? Why would I—"

"If Bronson set me up, did he do it on orders from your father?" I asked.

"No—I don't think so."

"Then he's acting for himself. Maybe he's rustling cattle from your father, and from Martinez, because he knows they'll accuse each other."

"Bronson?"

"Sure, he gets a few of the men to work with him and he starts a profitable little business on the side. Has your father ever admitted sending men across the river in retaliation?"

"No."

"Your father loses cattle, horses, but never gets any back. Martinez loses stock, but he never takes any back either. So where are all the missing animals?"

"Why are you asking me?"

"Because maybe Bronson has a partner. Maybe you're madder at your father than you admit."

"That's crazy," she said. "You think I want to ruin my father, that I set you up to be killed? You think I'm that kind of a person?"

"I don't know, Laura. Suppose you convince me you're not."

"And how do I do that? How do I make you believe me?"

"Take me out to the ranch, let me talk to Cletus Smith, or to Vern. I'll find out what I need to know from them."

"Aren't you afraid I'll lead you into a trap?"

"You won't have time. Take me tonight."

"Now?"

I nodded.

"If they catch you on the ranch—"

"Will your father have me killed?"

"Of course not!"

"If they catch me, they'll have to take me to him. If they kill me on his ranch, and they're doing what I think they're doing, it will bring too much attention to them. In any case, I'm willing to risk it."

"All right," she said after a moment's thought.

"Where's your horse?" I asked.

"At the livery."

"All right," I said, picking up my hat and rifle. "Let's go."

26

We rode out to the Kennedy ranch in the darkness, with
me following Laura very closely. She knew the way, and
we made very good time.

"Are there any guards?" I asked her.

"This is not an armed camp," she told me. "There are
guards on the herd, but not on the house and barn."

"Let's go to the barn, and we'll decide on how we're
going to move from there."

"Okay."

We rode up to the barn and I stayed in the shadows
while Laura opened it up. When the coast was clear, I
rode Duke into the barn and she closed the door behind
us.

I dismounted and we put the horses all the way in the
back, out of immediate sight.

"Now what?" she asked.

"Now you find out if Cletus or Vern are in the
bunkhouse, or out guarding the herd. I'll wait here."

"What if I come back with Bronson, and some men?"
she asked.

"That's up to you, Laura. I'm leaving myself in your
hands," I told her.

She stared at me for a long moment, then she reached
up and kissed me on the mouth.

"What's that for?" I asked.

"For trusting me."

I didn't tell her that there wasn't really any other choice in the matter. "Don't mention it. Go ahead, and be careful."

"Of what?" she asked. "I live here, remember?"

She slipped out and I found a place to sit and wait. She could very well come back with Bronson, Cletus, Vern, and some others, all ready to kill me. If that was the case, however, I was going to raise a hell of a ruckus and bring Enoch Kennedy running.

Which would all be very fine, as long as he wasn't with them.

I touched the .22 New Line inside my shirt for comfort, and then relaxed on my bale of hay and waited.

When the door started to swing open I got behind the hay bale and waited. It was Laura, and she was alone.

"Clint?" she called.

"Here," I said, stepping out into sight.

"This is strange," she said.

"What is?"

"Bronson, Vern, Cletus and a few of the others, they're not in the bunkhouse, but they're not with the herd, either."

I puzzled over it for a moment, too, and then realized that there was only one answer.

"That leaves only one other place they could be, Laura," I told her.

She stared at me, frowning, and then it seemed to dawn on her as well.

"The border?" she said.

"They must be grabbing some more cattle tonight."

"But from who?" she asked.

That was a very good question.

27

"What do we do now?" Laura asked.

Another good question. I was pretty sure Bronson and his men were stealing either Kennedy or Martinez cattle, but how could I know exactly where they would cross the Rio Grande? The possibilities here were too numerous to think out fully. If Kennedy were in on the whole thing, and Bronson was out stealing Martinez cattle, going to Enoch Kennedy would do no good. And if Kennedy was not in on it, would he believe me when I told him that his own foreman and men were stealing from him?

"You're going to have to stay here, Laura."

"What are you going to do?"

"I'm going back to town, and in the morning I'm going to try and get us some help."

"From who? The sheriff?"

I shook my head. "I don't know if I can trust the sheriff, Laura," I said.

"Well, aren't we going to try to stop the cattle thieves?" she asked.

"Chances are they've already cut the cows they want from the herd. We've got no way of knowing at what point in the river they're going to drive them across."

"We can't just do nothing," she argued.

"You're going to do nothing," I told her. "I'm going to do something. By morning, we'll know which cattle they took, Kennedy or Martinez, and then I can go from there."

"Go where?"

"Whoever's cattle they take tonight, the other one should be hit next. I'm going to have to try and find out when they'll hit next, and have help waiting there to grab them."

"That could take days, maybe weeks," she said.

"That's okay, Laura. If I can find the rustlers, I'll find the man who is trying to have me killed at the same time."

"Bronson?"

"I'm after the man Bronson is taking his orders from."

"My father?"

"I didn't say that, Laura, but you'll have to be prepared for that possibility."

"I suppose so."

I reached down and took her hand, hoping I was right in trusting her. "You won't hear from me for a while, Laura. Not until I have this thing figured out."

"Just take care of yourself, okay?"

"I will, I promise. You take care of yourself. Don't let Bronson or any of the others know that you suspect them."

"And don't tell my father?"

"Don't tell your father," I said. "Not unless you hear from me." I paused a moment, then added, "My life may depend on it."

She squeezed my hand and gave me a wan smile. "Vaya con Dios."

El Toro Rojo, Mexico
1873
PART II

28

El Toro Rojo, was much smaller and less busy than Lansdale. The buildings were a mixture of wood frame and adobe walls.

It was nearly noon when I rode in. I had left my wagon and team behind in Texas, choosing to ride into Mexico with Duke and whatever I could carry on me. All of my supplies were in my wagon, except for my gun, my rifle, and the .22 New Line in my shirt.

I rode to the livery first to put Duke up, and then booked a hotel room. After that I walked around, getting the lay of the town, and then stopped into the town's only cantina.

"Beer," I said to the bartender, who stared at me.

"Cerveca," said the man next to me.

The cantina was very small, barely large enough for the bar and ten or twelve tables. Aside from myself and the man standing next to me, there were two other people in the place, seated separately, nursing drinks.

I looked at the man next to me and said, "Thanks."

"No trouble," he said.

He was five-ten or so, in his early thirties, with a patch over his left eye. He hadn't shaved in days, or was growing a beard. On his left hip he wore a .44 Remington in a worn holster, and his clothes were of good quality, but dirty. He hadn't said enough for me to conclude whether he was American or Mexican, but he certainly looked Mexican.

The bartender brought me my "cerveca" and I took a sip and found it warm.

I'm never curious about other people, especially someone I've never met and am just having a momentary contact with, so I forgot about the man next to me and worked on forcing some of the warm beer down my throat to wash away the dust.

"Bartender, who is—" I started to ask, but then I remembered how much trouble I'd had ordering a beer.

"Can I be of service, Señor?" the man with the patch asked. He didn't turn his head or his body in my direction, he just stood the way he was and asked the question.

"I'd like to ask the bartender a question, if you would translate."

"It would be my pleasure to assist you," he said. "What is the question?"

"I'd like to know who the sheriff of this town is, and where I can find him," I told him.

He hesitated a moment, looking into his whisky glass and said, "I can answer that for you, Señor, but first I would like to ask a question of you."

"Go ahead."

"Why is it you wish to know who the sheriff of El Toro Rojo is? Most men, especially strangers, do not usually seek out the law when they first arrive in town."

"I do," I answered.

"I see," he said, examining his drink again. "I respect your right to answer as you choose, Señor, but I will strike a bargain with you."

"What kind of a bargain?"

"I will tell you the sheriff's name, and then you tell me why you wish to see him."

"And will I have to go elsewhere to get directions as to where I can find him?" I asked.

"I will tell you that, as well, Señor."

I examined his profile and it was very odd, because I couldn't see his eyes. You can usually read what's on a man's mind by examining his eyes, but all I could see was the patch covering his left eye.

"When I introduce myself to the sheriff, he might then understand why I wanted to see him and announce my presence in his town."

"Ah, you are an outlaw, perhaps? With a price on his head?" he asked.

"Are you a bounty hunter?"

"Please, Señor, do not insult me."

"Very well then," I said. "I am not an outlaw, but I have something of a reputation. I only wish to let the sheriff know I'm in town. I don't like games, Mister, so if you don't intend to answer my question, or translate it for me, I'll be moving on."

The stranger was annoying me now and I was ready to go looking for the sheriff myself.

"There is no need for you to go elsewhere, Señor," he said. "My name is Roberto Aguilar," he went on, finally turning to face me, showing me the star pinned to the right side of his shirt, "and I am the Sheriff of El Toro Rojo."

29

His lone eye was brown. That was the first thing I noticed, and then I realized that his badge *was* on the right side of his shirt. That fact hadn't really registered when he first turned towards me. I assumed that this had something to do with the fact that he was lefthanded.

"And now, Señor, that you have found the sheriff, would you be kind enough to introduce yourself?"

I turned to face the man with the patch and badge and said, "My name is Clint Adams."

The eyebrow over the black patch went up and I found myself wondering if that wasn't painful to him.

"You are correct, Señor Adams, in assuming that your reputation had preceded you. We here in Mexico are quite familiar with your fame as the Gunsmith."

"I didn't just assume it, Sheriff," I told him. "I was afraid of it."

"Is this true?"

"The reputation I have is not necessarily one I sought."

"You were a lawman for many years, were you not?"

"I was."

"And that explains why you wished to announce your arrival in Toro Rojo."

"I usually check in with the law when I arrive in a new town," I said.

"Ah, a good practice, I must say," the man with the patch agreed.

"Sheriff, could we go to your office?"

"Señor," he said, spreading his arms expansively, "we are in my office. If you will come with me, we can sit in that corner," he continued, pointing to a corner table. "Another beer?"

"If you've got any influence, I'd appreciate a cold one, this time."

"But of course, amigo," he said. He turned to the scrawny bartender and said something in rapid Spanish, the only word of which I understood being "cerveca."

I followed him to the corner table and as we approached it I said, "If you don't mind, Sheriff, I'd like to sit on the inside."

He smiled for the first time. "Of course, with your back to the wall. I understand, amigo. Please, my chair is your chair."

I sat down with my back against the wall and he sat opposite me.

"I have no worries," he announced to no one in particular. "I have a famous gunfighter to protect my back."

"I dislike that term," I said.

"I am sorry, Señor Adams. I did not mean to insult you."

"I guess that makes us even for my calling you a bounty hunter," I replied.

"Exactamente!"

The bartender came over with our drinks, and this time my beer was lukewarm.

"How is your cerveca, Señor?" the sheriff asked.

"We're getting closer."

His face resumed its initial grim lines and he said,

"Now, why have you come to my town, Señor?"

"Actually, I came in response to an invitation by Victor Martinez," I said, stretching the truth a bit.

"Ah, you are a friend of Don Victor?" the sheriff asked, the lines of his face relaxing into a smile for only the second time.

He seemed a strange combination of two men, with one face for each, the grim and the smiling.

"We are acquainted, yes. I have come to town to help him with his rustling problem."

"Ah, yes," Aguilar said, his face becoming grim again, which is when it seemed more natural. "The problem he has been having with Señor Kennedy from Texas."

"Are you sure it's Kennedy who's involved?" I asked.

"Who else could it be, Señor?"

Who else *could* it be? I thought I had at least half of the answer, now I wanted to find the other half. "I think I'll ride out and see Don Victor today," I said.

"Please send him my regards. Tell him that we do not see enough of him in town."

I got up and said, "I'll tell him. Thank you for your time, Sheriff."

"Anytime, Señor. If I can help Don Victor, you will let me know, eh?"

"I will let you know, Sheriff."

As I was leaving he was calling to the bartender, probably for another drink.

Sheriff Roberto Aguilar struck me as a very independant, very dangerous man. He looked mean, and no doubt the eyepatch loaned much to that facade, but he also seemed capable and clever. The smiling-sheriff was a convincing act. Whether or not he was in Victor Martinez's pocket was another matter. On the surface, it did not seem he would fit into anyone's pocket, but time would tell. Or maybe Martinez would tell me. I figured

I could be more open with Martinez than with Kennedy. At least, maybe nobody on Martinez's side would try to kill me.

At the livery I saddled up Duke, drawing funny looks from the liveryman.

"Sometimes plans change, big boy," I explained to Duke as we rode out of town, "and sometimes we don't have any plans at all, we just do what feels right. Understand?"

He didn't answer, but I knew he understood—which made one of us.

30

As I drove up to the Martinez house, I had some second
thoughts. What if Don Victor decided to blow me out of
the saddle as I rode up to his happy homestead?

I felt my stomach constrict as I got closer, but I was
too stubborn to stop, or turn around.

My fears were unfounded. When the door opened it
was not Don Victor's blazing guns but Lita Martinez's
blazing eyes that greeted me.

"Buenos dias."

"Hello, Lita."

She leaned on the porch railing, giving me a generous
view of the valley between her breasts, which overflowed
her low-cut blouse. "I knew you would come."

"How did you know that?"

"You cannot live without me," she said. "I knew it
after that night in your hotel room."

She looked as fiery, wild and lovely as ever, and if
Victor Martinez had not come through the front door at
that moment, all kinds of things could have happened
on that front porch.

"Ah, my amigo, Clint Adams. To what do we owe
this pleasant surprise?"

"I'd like to talk to you, if I may, Señor Martinez," I

said, tearing my eyes away from his daughter's dusky cleavage.

"Certainly, Señor Adams. I am glad you took up my offer to stop in any time."

"I'm glad you meant it."

"Shall we go inside?"

"All three of us?" Lita added, hands tucked impishly behind her back.

"I would like to talk to your father alone, Lita."

She pouted, making me want to bite into her lower lip right then and there, and then said, "Well, all right. I will be in the barn when you are finished. We can talk there."

"I'll be there."

I followed Victor Martinez inside and he said, "A drink?"

"Whatever you've got," I told him.

He produced a bottle of whisky and I told him, "Don't bother with the glasses. Just pass the bottle."

"Ah," he said, smiling, "then we are truly amigos."

"I'm counting on that, Señor—"

"Call me Victor."

"Then I'm counting on that, Victor," I repeated.

"That has an ominous sound, my friend," he said, passing me the bottle. "Can you explain why?"

I tipped the bottle, let some fire water down my throat, and then passed it back.

"I'll try to make this as clear and short as I can, and I may be taking my life in my hands by doing it."

"I assure you, my friend, you have nothing to fear from me," he said.

"I believe you, that's why I've come to offer my help."

"Ah, you will fight Señor Kennedy with me!" he exclaimed. "Bueno, very good—"

"That's not exactly what I mean."

"But, what else could you mean?"

I explained then, a partial theory, formed by Laura and myself—although I did not mention Laura.

"You believe a third party is stealing the cattle?" he said.

"I believe it's a possibility. Did you lose any cattle last night?"

"Why do you ask?"

"Did you?"

He took a swig from the bottle, but kept his eyes on me.

"I did not lose any cattle last night," he said, very deliberately, and then he hesitated again before saying, "but Señor Kennedy did."

"How do you know that?"

"First, how did you know that one of us would lose cattle last night?"

Now it was he who was suspicious of me, and I had to set his mind at rest before he'd talk to me anymore. I explained that I thought some of Kennedy's men were doing the rustling, taking from both sides, and that it was possible that Kennedy didn't know anything about it.

"Which men?" he asked. "We will take care—"

"No, no," I said, "we don't want to take care of them. We want to keep an eye on them and be ready for them the next time they strike."

"Why do we want to do that, Señor?" he asked.

"Because we want the man behind them. We want the man who started the rustling and then had one of his men try to kill me."

"You want the man who had you shot," he said, "you don't want to help me."

"That doesn't matter," I said, not bothering to deny his accusation. "I believe they are the same man. We can work together on this, Victor."

He thought a moment, cradling the bottle in both his

hands, and then said, "But it must be Kennedy, who else would—"

"Don't you see?" I asked. "If there is a third party, he was able to count on the fact that you two would naturally blame one another. Who would even think of looking for a third party?"

"And the men doing the rustling are actually Kennedy's men?"

"Some of his men, yes. I know of five, and two are dead."

"You killed them?"

"I killed one. The other was killed by his own people before I could get him to talk to me."

"But you do know the names of three of them?"

"I think so, yes," I said, "but there could be more."

"Yes?"

I stared at him and said, "Maybe on this side of the border."

He stared back for a moment, not understanding, and then when he did his eyebrows went up and he said, "My men? Impossible!"

"Yes, I know. They're all loyal."

"They are!"

"Especially Esteban, your foreman?"

"Esteban has been with me for years."

"Victor, do you know Enoch Kennedy's foreman?"

"Bronson. He has been with him for—" he started to say, then stopped short.

"For years, right?"

"His foreman?"

"And a few of his other 'loyal' workers. Think about it, okay?"

He passed me the bottle—which I assumed meant I was back in his good graces—and said, "Si, I will think."

"Good." I took a swig from the bottle and passed it

back to him again. "Now, tell me, how did you know that Kennedy was hit last night?"

"I have someone in Lansdale who sent word early this morning."

"Okay. That means you'll be next. Maybe days, maybe week—"

"You would wait that long?"

"When people start putting holes in me, I'll wait as long as it takes to return the favor."

"Yes," he said, examining me critically, "I believe you would, my friend."

"What about the sheriff in town? What's his name . . . Aguilar?"

"What about him?"

"Is he yours?"

"Mine? I do not—oh, I see. Does he work for me?"

"Does he work for you or the town? Can you trust him?"

"Well, he was elected by the town, of course. . . ." he said.

"But you did let it be known that you were backing him?"

"That is the case, yes."

"And you . . . pay him something."

"A small amount every month, just to be sure that my interests are looked after."

"Can you trust him?"

"Roberto?" he asked, smiling slightly. "I hope so. He is my nephew, my late sister's son. Yes, I believe I can trust him—at least as much as I trust you, Señor Clint."

"Just 'Clint,' please," I said. "If we are going to work together, that is."

"I will work with you, Clint," he explained, "until I find that it is no longer in my best interests to do so."

"That's agreeable," I said. I took a final drink from the bottle and gave it back. "I think it would be wise if you told your men I was staying here as your guest, and that I was free to roam your property."

"Did you ask Señor Kennedy for the same privileges?"

"Since I'm pretty sure some of his men are cattle rustlers, and that they want me dead, it wouldn't have been a healthy request."

"I will inform Esteban, and he will inform the remainder of the men. You will be safe on my property, Clint."

That was reassuring, but it wouldn't necessarily keep me from peeking over my shoulder every once in a while.

"I might as well return to town and pick up the gear I left in the hotel," I said, standing up.

"Do not forget that Lita is waiting in the barn to talk to you."

"Oh, yes. I'll stop in there before I go," I assured him.

"You seem to have made quite an impression on my daughter."

"She's a lovely girl. You're a very lucky man."

"So is the man who will eventually marry her," he said.

"I'm sure. I'll see you soon, Victor."

"I will have Lita make ready your room."

I nodded and left him to finish the bottle himself—not that there was much to finish. I was feeling a little light-headed from the liquor I'd consumed, and stopped on the porch to take a few deep breaths to clear my head.

"We'll be leaving soon, fella," I said, patting Duke's neck. "I have an appointment in the barn, first."

31

"Lita," I called.

"Here."

From that single word I was able to locate her, lying on a pile of hay, nude. Her wild mass of black hair was spread out all around her head, and the fingers of her right hand were avidly probing among the dark hairs between her legs.

"Come to me, Clint," she said, the movement of her fingers increasing. "I am ready."

As I approached, I caught a musky, sex-scent that indicated she was not only ready, but close to being finished.

"Lita—"

"First you must lie with me," she said, extending her arms, "and then we will talk."

The heady scent of her body, combined with the effect of the liquor, made her demands too much to resist. I dropped my gunbelt, shucked my clothes, and got into that haybed with her.

She was steaming hot. Her mouth, her tongue, the wetness that already waited for me between her legs, were all hot and eager.

When she had sucked me to an incredible hardness,

she straddled me and guided me into her to the hilt. She readied herself to ride me but I said, "Oh, no," and grabbed her buttocks firmly.

"What—" she began.

"I am not wounded, this time."

Holding her firmly I flipped her over and then drove myself as deeply into her as I could. Her breath caught in her throat and her legs wrapped around my waist.

"Oh, Dios. . ." she began to mutter over and over. She bit me on the neck and shoulders constantly as I drove myself into her. Her small hands gripped my buttocks as firmly as they could and her nails dug into my flesh.

"You trying to rip me apart?" I asked in her ear.

"You are tearing me apart!" she whispered urgently into mine.

"Do you mind?"

"Dios, no, I love it!" I continued to pound away at her, and she began to murmur, "More, more. . ." She kept saying it over and over, when her mouth wasn't busy taking little pieces out of me.

"Oh Jesus, Lita," I said as her muscles continued to milk me.

She laughed softly in my ear and said, "I have you, Clint, I have you and I will not let you escape."

"I'd have to be crazy to want to escape," I replied.

"I like talking during sex," she said, scraping my skin with her nails, "it makes it so much more . . . intimate."

"Oh, really?" I asked. "Well, how do you feel about screaming during sex?"

Before she could answer I lifted her buttocks up and rotated her hips as I continued to thrust into her. Her eyes went wide and her mouth opened, and before she could scream I plunged my tongue into her open mouth.

When she did scream it went directly into my mouth with a force that rattled my teeth.

"Oh, God," she said in a raspy voice when I freed her mouth. "Oh, Dios." She ran her hands through my hair, grabbing handfuls. "Ohhhh. . ." she moaned and suddenly she was bucking beneath me wildly as she climaxed. The force of it wrenched an orgasm from me that I'd had intentions of holding back. I thought it would never stop.

Finally, it did, and she stopped moving beneath me. Her mouth continued to work on my neck and shoulders and I said, "Just leave enough of me to put in a box."

"Mmmm," she said, "you are delicious."

"So are you, but now it's time to talk."

She pouted as she had earlier, and this time I did bite that lush, lower lip.

"Ouch!"

"That's what you get," I said, rolling off of her.

She looked at the drop of blood on her finger, than touched her lip again and said, "I liked it."

"You're bad," I said.

"I am a bad woman?"

"You are a very bad woman," I agreed.

"Good."

When we had gotten ourselves cleaned up and dressed she asked, "What did you and my father talk about? Did you ask for my hand in marriage?"

"I did not."

"Oh," she said, looking disappointed.

I buckled my gunbelt on and told her what her father and I had discussed.

"I agree," she said when she'd heard me out.

"With what?"

"With both decisions. Yours to trust my father, and his to trust you."

"Well, I'm glad we have your approval. Will you tell your father?"

She shook her head. "My approval would have no meaning to him."

"Maybe not."

"I will walk you to your horse," she said.

We left the barn and walked to Duke, with her hand on my arm all the way. As I started to mount up she yanked on my arm, spinning me around. She threw her arms around my neck and kissed me soundly on the lips.

"It will be nice having you stay with us, Clint."

"Thanks," I said, patting her behind and climbing up on Duke.

"It will be like having a brother in the house."

32

I went back to Toro Rojo, collected my gear from the hotel, and checked out.

"A short stay, Señor," said the clerk as he accepted my money.

"I have found better accommodations."

"But, Señor," he said, looking puzzled, "there are no better accommodations in Toro Rojo."

I went out front and threw my saddlebags on Duke's back. As I was securing them Sheriff Aguilar—Victor Martinez's nephew—walked over.

"Ah, Señor Adams, you are leaving Toro Rojo already? We have done something to displease you, perhaps?"

"Not at all, Sheriff," I assured him. "Don Victor has invited me to be a guest in his house. I could not refuse his generous hospitality."

"Of course not. I do not blame you. I hope that you will be of great assistance to my—to Don Victor, Señor. Please, once again send him my best regards."

"Of course," I said, mounting up. "It was a pleasure meeting you, Sheriff. I hope to see you again."

"I am sure you will, Señor," he said. "Adios."

"Adios," I repeated, and started off down the street.

For some reason my back started to itch, but I refrained from looking back.

I could have been picked off from any doorway, window, or rooftop. I took a deep breath and didn't let it out until I was safely out of town.

I was on Victor Martinez's land when I heard the shot and felt something fly by my head. For an instant I was torn between jumping to the ground and sending Duke off at a gallop. With less horse under me, I don't think I would have tried to outrun a bullet, but with Duke I figured to give it a shot. "Let's go, big fella."

As Duke took his initial jump there was another shot and a bullet whizzed through the space that only moments before had been occupied by my head. In my mind's eye I could see the rifleman tracking me with his sight, and I could see the surprise on his face as Duke continued to accelerate. He took another shot that was way off, and then we were gone.

Duke continued to eat up ground with those gigantic strides of his and I let him have his head all the way to Martinez's house. They heard him coming on the house and were out on the porch as I rode up—Martinez, Lita, and Esteban.

I reined Duke in and hopped down to the ground.

"You are in such a hurry, my friend," Martinez said, "We would have saved you some dinner had you arrived later."

"Food was not on my mind, Victor," I told him, "but saving my neck was."

I told them what had happened on the trail and kept my eyes on Esteban, the foreman of Martinez's ranch, the whole time.

"Now, when did you tell your men about me?" I asked Victor.

"I have only just now told Esteban of your presence," he answered.

"That's right," Lita said, backing him up.

Esteban stayed silent and studied me with distrust in his eyes.

"So it couldn't have been any of your men shooting at me?" I said.

"That is correct," Esteban said. "The patron has only just informed me of your presence."

"Yeah." We locked eyes and stayed that way for a few long moments, and then I said, "I'll take care of my horse and join you in the house."

"Dinner will be waiting," Victor assured me.

"I will help you," Lita said, stepping down from the porch as the two men went back into the house.

"You are not hurt?" Lita asked, as we walked back to the barn we'd left just hours ago.

"No, I'm not hurt," I answered, "thanks to the big boy, here." I patted Duke's neck affectionately.

"He is beautiful," she said, putting a hand on his hind quarters. He didn't usually like being touched by other people, but he tolerated the touch of her hand.

"You've got good taste," I said into his ear.

He tossed his head and I patted his neck again.

"You talk to him?" she asked.

"Sure, he's my best friend," I explained. "We've been through a lot together, me and Duke."

In the barn I stripped his gear off, brushed and fed him while Lita watched, sprawled on the same bunch of hay we'd been on before.

"Mmmm," she said, holding a handful of hay to her face. "This hay smells special."

She had a way about her, that little girl. Holding the hay to her nose, staring at me with those eyes, I started to get hard again. She saw it and started to pull her skirt up to her thighs.

I reached down, grabbed her elbows and pulled her to her feet.

"I don't want to keep your father and his foreman, waiting, Lita."

"All right, but I'll come to your room later tonight," she promised.

"We'll see." I gripped her elbows tightly. "I'll let you know."

She stared at me boldly, and then her gaze changed and she said, "Yes, Clint."

She needed strong handling, this little girl. The man who married her had better be ready to give it to her, or she'd break him like a cowboy breaking an untamed wild horse.

She was a wild filly, full of fire and life—and beautiful. She was unbroken, and I had no intentions of trying to break her, but I figured while I was here, I might as well go for a ride or two.

"Come on," I said, "let's have dinner. All of a sudden I'm hungry."

"So am I," she said, but her eyes told me that hers was a different kind of hunger.

33

The tension between Esteban and me didn't ruin Victor's or Lita's appetites, but it played havoc with ours. Also, Mexican food isn't exactly my favorite, so I didn't really mind swapping stares with Esteban instead of eating.

"You two hombres are ruining my dinner," Victor Martinez said, suddenly putting his fork down.

"You couldn't tell by me," I commented.

"You have been eying each other like two roosters. If we are to work together, Clint, than you will have to work with Esteban. I trust him."

Esteban lifted his chin and stared down his nose at me.

"And you, hombre," Victor went on, staring at Esteban. "This man did not have to offer his help, but he did, and I have accepted. That means that you must work with him." He split his attention between the two of us then and said, "That is the way it is to be."

Esteban tore his eyes away from mine, looked at Martinez and said, dutifully, "Si, Patron."

"Have you finished with your food?" Martinez asked him.

"Si, Patron."

"Then you have work to do."

"Si, Patron."

The foreman threw me one last suspicious glance then got up from the table, said good night to Lita, and left. The way his eyes lingered on Lita told me something, also. Another reason why maybe Esteban was less than thrilled to see me around.

A reason why he might like to see me stop a bullet, which had nothing to do with loyalty to the Patron.

When Esteban left, Victor said, "Now, go ahead, eat."

"I've had enough, thanks," I told him.

"Then it should not go to waste." He reached over and scraped the contents of my plate into his.

Lita stood up, took my empty plate, and said, "I will bring you coffee."

When she left the room I leaned over and asked her father in a low voice, "Has something been going on between Esteban and Lita?"

He looked up at me with his mouth full of food, took time to chew and swallow, and then said, "There was something going on, yes."

"Was?"

"Si. Since the first day you were here, however, Lita has not been very kind to Esteban."

"I see."

He poked at his food, then put his fork down and looked at me again.

"I think I see," he said. "You think that perhaps Esteban is jealous, and would like to see you dead."

"I think that perhaps your daughter is what will keep Esteban and me from working together. He may not distrust me, but he sure as hell doesn't like me, and she's the reason."

"I am the reason for what?" she asked, returning with a pot of coffee.

"Put the coffee pot down and go, girl," her father told her.

"Papa—" she started to protest.

"Andale! This is man talk. It does not concern you."

She stared at him for a moment, and I thought she might dump the coffee into his lap, but finally she put the pot on the table, turned and flounced out of the room.

"She should have been a man, that one," he said, staring after her. "She has spirit, and is stubborn."

I didn't argue, although I much preferred Lita as a woman. So, I was sure, did Esteban, which brought us back to the problem at hand.

"What about Esteban?" I asked.

"It is no secret that Esteban would like to marry my Lita," he said.

"Do you approve?"

"Esteban is a very good foreman," he replied, "but I do not think he would be a suitable husband, or son-in-law."

"Have you told him that?"

"I have not."

"I thought you said you trusted him, that he was loyal? You think telling him that he's not good enough for your daughter would change that?"

He looked down at his food, but seemed to have lost his appetite. "I suppose one should not trust so blindly."

"Not when there are so many conditions, Don Victor," I commented. "I think it would be unwise at this point to let Esteban know everything that I will be doing. Let's keep him in the dark for a little while."

"Eh?"

"Let's just keep certain matters between ourselves for a while."

"Very well. What will your moves be, then?"

"We know they picked up some cows last night. I'm going to try and find out at which point they came across the river with them. They can't very well have covered up that many tracks overnight."

"Do you want a man to ride with you?"

"No, I'll ride alone. I'll let you know what I come up with."

"Clint, you may be being too careful," he said.

"How so?"

"You need someone who knows the country. You can't ride alone. What if you get lost?"

"I won't get lost, Victor, but I do see your point."

I rubbed my jaw and thought it over. He had a point, all right. Having someone with me who knew the area would be a big help.

"All right," I agreed. "I'll take somebody with me."

"Esteban?" he asked, and then he shook his head and answered his own question, "No."

"No. I'll take—"

"What about Roberto?" he asked. "He can—"

"No, Victor," I said, interrupting him. "I know who I want."

"Who?"

It might antagonize Esteban even more, but it couldn't be helped. The simple fact of the matter was I didn't trust anyone else as much as I trusted—

"Lita."

34

We started out on horseback the next morning, heading for the river.

"Where will we start?" Lita asked as we saddled up.

"Where the herd is, and work our way towards the border. The rustlers must have someplace on either side of the Rio Grande where they've been stashing the stolen cows until they're ready to move them."

She smiled at me and swung into her saddle, sitting her horse as if she were feeling no effects from the whole night we'd spent pounding away at each other. I admitted I was sore, but I didn't show it either as I mounted Duke. The look on her face said she knew it, though.

I also knew now that, even if I wanted to try, I'd never be able to break her. She had too many years and too much energy on me.

"Let's go," she said.

"Lead on."

We spent the better part of the morning riding up and down the banks of the Rio Grande, looking for tracks, first on the Texas side, and then on the Mexico side.

"Here," I said, finally, on the Mexico side. Lita rode up next to me and I pointed to the ground. "They kept them as strung out as possible—see here, two by two—

to make the tracks as unnoticeable as possible. Walk them in a straight line rather than let them bunch up."

"I understand."

"Now all we've got to do is follow these tracks," I told her. "We find out where they're hiding their cows, and who is guarding them, we'll find out who's involved —on the Mexico side, that is."

As we rode along with the tracks she said, "If I understand this correctly, you believe that someone from Señor Kennedy's ranch and someone from Papa's ranch are working together, stealing cattle from both ranches?"

"You're a smart girl."

"I know it. You suspect Esteban?"

"I don't know, Lita. Was he really with you and your father yesterday while I was being shot at?"

"Yes, he was, Clint."

"He loves you, you know that, don't you?"

She looked thoughtful and said, "I suppose."

"Who are the men loyal to, Lita, Esteban or your father?" I asked her.

"My father, of course," she answered.

"Think about it. There must be a few men who Esteban himself brought to the ranch, who are loyal to him. Think."

We rode along in silence for a while as she turned it over in her mind.

"All right," she said, finally. "There are one or two men who Esteban hired without my father's okay."

"And maybe a couple others he offered money to," I added.

"To steal cows?"

"Or to kill me, because of you."

"He might have paid someone to kill you, but not necessarily to steal cows," she said.

"Or the other way around."

I pulled up short and examined the ground.

"What is wrong?" she asked.

"They started brushing out the tracks here."

"Can't you find them?" she asked.

"I'm no expert." By keeping the cows strung out the way they did, they were able to erase the tracks—to some extent. There must have been stragglers, though.

"Move out to your left, Lita. Look for tracks. They couldn't have kept all those cows together the whole time."

I moved left while she moved right, and eventually I found some signs I could read. We'd go along for a while, lose the tracks, spread out again, and then one of us would find the trail of another straggler. We were making progress, even though it was taking a while.

"Let's rest your horse," I told her at one point.

"What about yours?" she asked, dismounting.

I patted Duke's neck and said, "He's fine. This has been nothing more than a stroll for him."

I looked around at the countryside, from where we'd come, and where we were headed.

I pursed my lips and let the air out in a rush, making a sound of disgust.

"What is wrong?" she asked, looking up at me.

I pointed back the way we'd come, and moved my finger and pointed to where we were going.

"Are we headed where I think we are?" I asked.

She looked in both directions, and then said, "If we keep going in this direction, we will reach the ranch."

"And before that?"

She stared at me, then said, "The herd."

"The herd," I repeated.

She mounted up again and said, "Why? What is wrong?"

"Oh, nothing's wrong," I told her. "In fact, it's beau-tiful."

"What is?"

"Where they've been hiding the stolen cows."

"Where?" she asked, looking lost.

"Where nobody would notice them," I answered. "Who's going to notice a hundred head or so when you're dealing with thousands."

"I don't—"

"Your father's herd, Lita," I explained. "They've been hiding the stolen cows in with your father's herd— and probably doing the same thing on the other side with Kennedy's herd. Yeah, it's beautiful."

We rode along in silence for a while and then I said, "Yeah, where better to hide a tree than in a forest?"

"What?" she asked.

"Nothing," I said. "Never mind. It wasn't anything very important."

"Wouldn't anyone notice the different brand?" Lita asked as we continued to follow the tracks.

"Not if they didn't want to," I told her. "Who assigns the men who are to guard the herd?" I asked.

"Esteban."

"And I'll bet the same men usually pull that job, don't they?"

"I don't know."

"Well I do. And your father, how often does he go out to inspect the herd?"

"He doesn't. He leaves that to Esteban."

Esteban again. More and more it began to look like Esteban and Bronson were working on this thing together. Still, I didn't think either one of them was the brains behind the scheme. There was somebody else giving the orders, and that was the man I wanted.

35

When we came to within sight of the herd, I told Lita to stop.

"I found out what I needed to know," I told her. "No need to go any further."

"Shall we tell Papa?"

I eyed the herd as I thought it over. I guessed we might as well tell Victor, and maybe Aguilar, too. I had to dissuade them from taking any action, though. Not yet, anyway. We had Esteban and his boys on the Mexico side, and Bronson and his boys on the Texas side. We still needed the man in charge, though.

"Let's go to the house," I told her. "I want to talk with your father."

She shrugged and followed me to the house. We found Martinez sitting at his desk, involved in paperwork. I was glad to see that. I was starting to wonder how he kept his ranch running if all he did was eat and drink.

I sat in a chair in front of his desk and said, "I think I've got most of it figured out."

He put down the papers he'd been examining, looked at Lita and said, "You can go, Lita. This is—"

"Let her stay, Victor. She knows as much as I do. She's a bright girl."

She gave her father a haughty look and he said, "Very well. You may stay."

Delighted, she sat in another chair and paid attention.

I described how we'd picked up the tracks and followed them to his herd, explained that that was where they were hiding the stolen cows.

"In my herd?" he asked, indignantly.

"Just for a short time, probably. Until they could cover their tracks."

"Why didn't Roberto ever find these tracks?" he wondered aloud.

"Oh, I wouldn't blame him. He probably didn't relish getting up early and leaving his office to ride around the countryside looking for cow tracks."

"I pay him to look out for my interests," he said.

"Do you still trust him?" I asked.

He thought a moment.

"Well, I suppose he is lazy and no good, but I don't believe he would steal from me."

"Okay, then we'll let him in on this. He's the law, but I don't want any action taken, yet."

"Why not?"

I hesitated a moment, then said, "I'd like to set up a meeting between you and Kennedy."

"Kennedy," he said, shaking his head. Then he stopped and mulled it over.

"You may still have reasons to feud, but the rustling is no longer one of them. We'll all have to work together on this, Victor. The law on this side, and the law in Texas." I leaned forward and added, "And I still want the man behind it all."

"Very well," he agreed. "Where and when?"

"I'll let you know. I've got to set it up with Kennedy, first. I'm going to have to convince him. I'll take Lita to Texas with me and send her back with the information."

"Lita?"

"I'll take care of her."

"I will be fine, Papa," she assured him, itching to go.

"All right. I suppose we must resolve this matter finally," he agreed.

"Get a fresh mount, Lita," I instructed her.

She jumped up and I said, "Take your time. We'll give Duke a while to get rested."

She nodded, and hurried out.

"Esteban," Victor said, half to himself.

"It's got to be, Victor," I said. "He sets the guards up on the herd, makes sure they're his men. Bronson must do the same on the Kennedy herd. It wouldn't work if the two foremen weren't in on it."

"I suppose not," he said.

I got up and said, "I'll pack my gear and meet Lita out front. With any luck, she'll be back here tomorrow with the time and place for the meeting."

"Do you think Señor Kennedy will agree?" he asked.

"If he's a smart man, he will," I replied. "I'm sure he wants the rustling to come to an end just as much as you do."

"I hope so," he said.

I packed my saddlebags and was throwing them on Duke's back when Lita came out of the barn with her fresh mount.

"Ready?" she asked.

"Yes."

She touched my arm. "Thank you for taking me along, Clint."

"You're the only one I can trust to bring the message back, Lita."

"If Señor Kennedy agrees."

"He will," I said, confidently. "I'll have some help convincing him," I said, thinking of Laura.

"His daughter?" she asked.

"How did you know that?" I asked.

She gave me a coy look and said, "Knowing you, it was easy to guess."

TEXAS
Part III

36

We bypassed Lansdale and rode straight to the Kennedy spread. It was getting late in the day, and there wasn't much activity around the main house. A couple of hands gave us the eye, but no one seemed to recognize me, and I didn't know any of them.

We stopped in front of the front door and Lita tied her horse off. I left Duke loose, knowing he wouldn't go anywhere without me. When I knocked on the door, it was answered by Laura.

"Clint," she said in surprise. When she saw Lita she stared. Sparks passed between the eyes of the two women, but they were not like the sparks that pass between a man and a woman.

"What is she doing here?" Laura demanded.

"Then you know who this is," I said.

"Victor Martinez's daughter," she said.

"Lita, this is Laura Kennedy."

"I know."

"Well, now that that's settled, I'd like to see your father, Laura. I've got a lot to tell him."

"I'll bet," she said. "You've probably been very busy in Mexico, haven't you?"

"I have, indeed," I said. "Take us to your father, Laura, please."

She hesitated, then said, "He's in the study. Come on."

I closed the door behind us and we followed Laura to the study. Lita was examining Laura from the back, as only one woman can examine another.

"Behave," I said to her under my breath. She stuck her tongue out at me and smiled broadly. She was enjoying Laura's anger.

Laura opened the door to her father's study without knocking and said, "Father, Clint Adams is here to see you."

As I entered the room Enoch Kennedy stood up behind his desk.

"What are you doing here?" he demanded. "And who is she?"

"Father," Laura said, "this is Victor Martinez's daughter."

Kennedy stared at Lita and said, "What the hell is she doing here? What's the meaning of this, Adams?"

"If you'll sit down and relax, Mr. Kennedy, I'll explain it to you. I've got the answer to your rustling problem."

"I don't care—I don't believe—"

"Your daughter knows I have the answer, Mr. Kennedy," I told him, and then looked to Laura for help. She was standing with her arms folded across her chest, and for a moment I thought she would allow her obvious jealousy and anger to interfere, but finally she spoke up.

"I think you should listen to him, Father," she said.

"If you really want to solve the problem, that is," I put in.

"All right, I'll listen to you," Kennedy said, sitting back down.

I sat in front of his desk, and Lita and Laura sat at

opposite ends of the room.

I ran the whole thing down for him, telling him how the foreman of each ranch was in on the rustling, bringing with them whatever men they could sway.

"They're stealing from both of you, Mr. Kennedy," I explained, "knowing that you would each blame each other and not look elsewhere for a guilty party—and it worked."

"That's preposterous," he replied. "Deke Bronson wouldn't do such a thing. He's like my own son."

I told him about meeting Bronson, and how he left two men behind to finish me. "I have no doubt now that it was he or one of his men who shot me that day by the border, and killed your man Dobbs to keep him from talking to me."

"I can't believe this."

"Mr. Kennedy, if you would have me believe that you have nothing to do with stealing Martinez cattle, that you are not doing so in retaliation—"

"That would make me the same as him," he interrupted me.

"All right, then. You're not having your men steal his cattle and he's not having his men steal yours—but they are. At least, some of them are, and they're hiding the stolen cattle among your own herd."

"What?"

"When they steal from you, they hide them in Martinez's herd, and when they steal from him, they hide them with yours. It's easy enough to check," I told him.

He wasn't so sure anymore that what I was saying was so unbelievable.

"Kennedy, it wouldn't work if the foremen weren't involved. They put their own men on the herds so that no one else will notice the different brands."

"Bronson. . ." he murmured, staring into space.

"And Vern, and Cletus Smith, and probably a few others."

He compressed his lips, and then his eyes focused on me once again.

"I'll send for the sheriff."

"That's another thing. Can you trust him?"

"He works for me," Kennedy said. "Aside from the fact that he looks out for my interests, he's been a good lawman."

"All right, then, but I have a better idea."

"What?"

"I don't think Bronson, or Esteban, the Martinez foreman, are the brains behind this."

"Who then?"

"That's what I want to know," I replied, "because that's the man who had me shot in the back."

"What do you suggest, then?"

"I want to set up a meeting between you, Martinez and your two sheriffs. Let's make some plans, Kennedy, so that the next time they hit, we can be ready for them. Once we catch them in the act, maybe they'll give us the big man's name. What do you say?"

He rubbed his jaw, and said, "All right, Adams, I'll go along with you, but how do we know when they'll hit next?"

"We don't know when, but I think we know where. In the morning send for Sheriff Cross. I'll send Lita back to Mexico to tell her father where and when we'll meet. He'll bring Sheriff Aguilar, from Toro Rojo. Meanwhile, we'll spend the night here."

"Oh, really?" Laura asked.

"Have rooms prepared for them," Kennedy told her.

"Two?" she asked, sarcastically.

"Go on, Laura," he snapped.

"Yes, Father."

"There were two men out front when I rode in," I said quickly, before she could leave the room.

"Hartman and Barker," Laura said.

"They're my men," Kennedy said. "They don't even like Bronson."

"I hope you're right," I said. I turned to Laura and said, "Have them take care of our horses, and tell them to hide Duke as best they can. If Bronson sees him he'll know I'm in the house."

Laura nodded and left the room.

"You had better be right about all of this, Adams," Kennedy told me.

"I am, Mr. Kennedy, and I think you know it."

"We'll see," he said, getting up and walking around the desk to the door. "You can both wait here. Laura will show you to your rooms."

When Kennedy left Lita said, "Why did you not tell her to prepare one room?"

"We don't need that kind of trouble tonight, Lita. When I put you in your room, you stay there, do you hear me?"

"I hear you," she said.

"You'd better do it."

"I will stay in my room, Clint," she said, raising her right hand. "I promise."

I wished I could believe her, but I had this feeling of dread that if Laura and Lita ended up in the same place at the same time, I might not make it through the night alive.

37

Laura showed us to our rooms, stopping first at Lita's.

"This is your room, dear," she told Lita sweetly.

"And where is Clint's?" Lita asked, in a tone just as sweet.

Laura hesitated a moment, then pointed down the hall and said, "Second door on the right—and how did I know you would ask that question?"

"We are women," Lita told her, and then turned to me and said, "Good night, Clint."

"Good night, Lita. Remember what I told you. I'll see you in the morning."

"It shall be as you wish," she told me, and then disappeared inside her room.

"Follow me," Laura said to me coldly, and led the way down the hall. At the second door on the *left* she stopped and opened it.

"Laura," I scolded her, "you told Lita the second door on the right."

We were in my room now and she turned to me and gave me a wicked smile and said, "Well, that's *my* room. It was an honest mistake."

Sure, I thought. I only hoped that Lita would do as I told her and stay in her own room all night.

"Laura—" I began, but she cut me off vehemently.

"Damn you, Clint Adams, for bringing that slut into my house," she said, pounding me on the chest. She was a big, strong girl and when she swung again I had no choice but to stop her.

"Laura, come on," I said, catching her wrist. "I had no choice."

"Why, did you need a little on the trail to help you make it?" she demanded, eyes flashing. She swung her other fist at me and I caught that one, too. Now I was holding both of her wrists and she began to struggle mightily.

"If you'll calm down, I'll explain," I told her. We started to stagger around the room as she fought to escape from my grip, and I fought to keep from being hit again.

"Let go!" she snapped.

"Not until you calm down," I told her.

Eventually, I got her worked over towards the bed. The back of her knees struck the mattress and she went down on her back, with me on top of her.

"Ow, you're hurting me," she said, squirming beneath me.

I was lying on the cushion of her breasts and thighs and her breath was coming in sharp gasps against my face as she continued to fight me.

"Laura, damn it—"

Suddenly she reached up and tried to bite me on the bottom lip. I pulled my head back in time, and then as her head hit the mattress again I covered her mouth with mine. She tried to protest, but I put my tongue in her mouth and pinioned her arms to the bed. Gradually, her struggles ceased, and her tongue came sweetly into my mouth. I released her hands and we were caught up in a totally different struggle, a struggle to get out of our clothes without breaking bodily contact. Soon we were pressing our naked bodies together.

The heat of her loins was intense. I kissed her again and she reached between us to take hold of me firmly. I returned the favor by sliding one hand between her legs and dipping my fingers into the wet depths of her. Her hips came off the bed to meet the thrust of my hand, and she began to rub me the length of my shaft.

"Oh, Clint," she said against my mouth, "you bastard, you dirty . . . rotten . . . oh!"

I touched her nub and she shuddered violently. I broke our mouth-to-mouth contact, removed my fingers and replaced them with my penis. I slid easily into her, and she wrapped her legs around me, murmuring, "Rotten . . . rotten . . . bastard—"

I silenced her with my mouth, and began to take her in long, slow strokes. I probed her insides in every possible direction, and she met every stroke with a strong thrust of her powerful hips.

Where Lita's beauty was fiery, Laura's was cool. The Mexican girl was almost ferocious, the American girl controlled, up until the moments before she was ready to come. Then she exploded into a flurry of activity. This time she lifted me off the bed with incredible strength, using her muscles to suck me in as I emptied myself into her.

"God, oh God," she moaned as I continued to fire my seed into her. She kept me inside of her, kept driving against me until she achieved another long moment of satisfaction, and then we lay still, regaining the breath we had first lost struggling, and then again making love.

"You weren't gone long," she said eventually.

"I found out what I needed to know surprisingly fast."

"You weren't gone long," she repeated, "but I missed you. I was waiting for you to come back, and then you show up with . . . with . . . her!"

"She was the only one I could trust not to shoot me in the back, Laura."

"How could she shoot you in the back if you kept her on hers?" she asked.

"Don't be bitchy," I said.

She threw me a look, her eyes flashing with anger, and then she stared at the ceiling.

"Laura, she's going to help bring this feud between your father and hers to an end."

"Will it? Will it end?"

"Well, if it doesn't, it won't be because of the cattle rustling," I said. "That will stop, and soon," I assured her.

She forced her anger aside for the moment and said, "Oh, I hope so, Clint, but. . ." and then trailed off.

"But what?" I asked.

She tore her eyes away from the ceiling and looked into mine and said, "But when it is over, you'll be moving on, won't you?"

"Yes, I will," I answered. "I'd never lie to you about that, Laura. I'd never try and make you believe—"

"That you love me?" she asked.

I nodded, and she smiled at me.

"I know that, Clint," she said. "You may be a rotten bastard sometimes, but you're an honest bastard."

"Thanks . . . I think."

She rolled over and mashed her large breasts against my chest and said, "Yes, it was a compliment."

I reached around and grasped the cheeks of her behind and began to knead them firmly. She closed her eyes and moaned, dropping her forehead against my chin. I kissed the top of her head and said, "You are the biggest girl. . ."

"Thanks," she said against my throat, "I think."

I slid one finger along the crack in her ass until I was

able to slide it between her vaginal lips and said, "Yes, that was a compliment."

"Ummm," she said as I probed deeper with my finger, as deep as I could in that position without pulling a muscle in my arm or shoulder. She began to ride my finger up and down, rubbing her body against me in the process. Trapped between us, my penis began to come back to life. She began to kiss my chest, then slid down and continued downward. She kissed my ribs, my belly, kept going until she was kissing and biting my inner thighs. Her fingers were teasing my scrotum, cupping my balls in her hand and then licking them. She slid them into her mouth gently, first one and then the other, and then concentrated her attention on my incredibly hard erection. Her tongue came out and encircled the swollen head and I closed my eyes to the sensations. When she allowed me to slip into her mouth I thought I would come right there and then, but I held on. She took as much of my shaft into her mouth as she could and began to suck, cheeks hollowing out, head bobbing up and down as she drew me to the brink of completion.

"Come up here," I whispered, running my hands over her back, and then beneath her. I cupped her large breasts and used them to draw her back up to me.

Instead of lying atop me she sat up on me, raised her hips, and took me inside of her. She remained sitting, head thrown back, breasts thrust out, riding me up and down. I reached her breasts and squeezed them hard enough to leave fingermarks. I tweaked her nipples as she continued to swallow me up, sliding me in and out with ever increasing speed. When I could take no more I reached for her, pulled her close to me and then turned us over, so that I was on top.

"Yes," she said into my ear, "Yes, oh yes. . ."

I began to suck her breasts as I worked myself in and out of her warmth. I would slam myself deep into her, then pull out until my tip almost popped loose, then ram it home again. All the time she was moaning and clutching at me, saying, "Yes, please, oh please, don't stop, never stop. . ."

I never wanted to stop, either, but that was beyond my power. I emptied myself into her with such intensity that it was exquisitely painful.

"Oh, God," she said, into my ear. "I don't want you to leave, I never want you to leave." She held me tightly to her.

"Laura—"

"Don't say anything, Clint. I want to fall asleep with you inside me. You still feel so big, so comfortable in there. Please, can we do that?"

"Of course," I said, kissing her neck. I only hoped that Lita didn't come looking for me and find that Laura had given her the wrong directions.

I was ready to sleep for a long time, on the firm cushions of Laura's marvelous body, and I didn't want anything or anybody to interfere with that.

38

In the morning we picked out a meeting place that would be easy for all involved to find.

"Lita, do you know a deep arroyo on this side of the border," I asked her, "between Lansdale and the river?"

"Si, I know it."

"Good. Have your father and Roberto Aguilar meet us there at three this afternoon."

"Comprendo, Clint."

I turned to Kennedy and asked, "Is that all right with you?"

"That's fine," he said. "Do we bring any men?"

"Not yet. It will just be Martinez, Sheriff Aguilar, you, Sheriff Cross, and me."

"And me," Lita said.

"And me," Laura added.

I looked at each of them in turn and decided not to argue about it.

To Kennedy I said, "Seven of us, that's enough of a crowd."

"All right."

"Meanwhile, you might start thinking about just how many of your men *are* your men," I told him. "How many you can trust. Lita, tell your father to do the same. We have to get some idea of how large a force we can put together. Get going.''

"Walk me to my horse?" she asked.

I saw Laura's face cloud over, but I agreed.

"I disobeyed you, last night," Lita told me, proudly as we left the house.

"Oh?"

"I left my room and followed the directions that the Americano woman gave me. You were not in that room."

She did not seem angry, but amused.

"It was her room," she said, "but she was not there, either."

"I see."

We reached her horse, which was saddled and ready, and she turned to me and said, "Do you like this woman, with the tits as big as a cow's?"

"I like all women."

"I understand, Señor," she assured me, giving me a saucy, teasing look. She turned and raised one foot for me to give her a boost up. I did so, but as her tight little rear came level with my head I gave her a resounding slap on the fanny with my right hand.

"Ow!" she squealed, staring down at me darkly from the saddle.

"That is for disobeying me last night," I told her. "Disobedient girls get spanked. Remember that, too."

She leaned over and rubbed her rump, then smiled at me and said, "Oh, I will remember, Señor. Adios."

"Until three," I reminded her.

"Si, until three."

I watched her as she rode away, and then returned to the house. Laura met me just inside the door. I couldn't tell if she had been watching or not.

"A fond farewell?" she asked, sarcastically.

"Let's go back to your father," I suggested.

When we returned to Enoch Kennedy's study he was

seated at his desk staring down at something he had written on a piece of paper, and he was shaking his head.

"What's wrong, Father?" Laura asked.

He looked up at us and his eyes seemed haunted, sunken in. He looked older.

"This is upsetting," he said. "I have attempted to make a list of men I know I can trust," he told us. "Once, Deke's name would have been right at the top of the list. I employ forty men on this ranch, Mr. Adams. Do you know how many names I've written here? Three!" He continued to shake his head.

"Well, Mr. Kennedy, if it's any comfort to you, I doubt that Bronson would have cut that many men in on the deal. I figure he had Dobbs, and Fred, who are dead, and he's got Vern and Clete Smith, maybe a couple of others. Esteban probably has five or six men, as well. I don't think we'll be dealing with more than ten men."

At least, that's what I was hoping.

"Laura, I've decided to ride into town myself and talk to Sheriff Cross. Would you like to come with me and help me convince him?"

"Sure," she said. "I'll go saddle up."

"I'll saddle Duke myself," I called after her.

"All right."

"Do you think it would help if I sent Amos a message by telegraph?" Kennedy asked.

"It might, at that," I said. "Why don't you tell him that I'm coming to town and that I'm acting on your behalf. I may get a better reception that way."

"Very well."

"And keep working on that list," I told him. "Get at least five or six names, but don't say anything to them until I get back."

"All right."

"We'll be back in plenty of time, sir."

"I'll be ready."

I went out to the barn, where Laura was almost done saddling her horse, and got Duke ready.

"Laura, how well do you know Amos Cross?" I asked.

"Not well," she said. I looked over at her and she said, "No, really, Clint. I don't like small men, and he doesn't like big girls. We got that out of the way right at the beginning, when father hired him."

"Hired him?"

"Well, had him hired, then. Father recommended him for the job as sheriff, and that was enough to get Amos elected. He's been a good sheriff, too."

"Well, I only hope he's good enough to believe what I'm going to tell him," I said, mounting up. "We'll need his authority on this."

"He'll help," she said, confidently. "As long as he knows it's what Father wants."

"I hope you're right," I said. "Let's go."

39

We found Amos Cross in his office, with Kennedy's telegram spread out in front of him. He looked up and watched us with careful eyes as we approached his desk.

"Miss Kennedy," he said, greeting Laura respectfully. He looked at me with something akin to distaste and asked, "What's this all about, Adams?" He waved the telegram in his hand to show me what he was referring to.

"It will take a bit of explaining, Sheriff," I told him.

"I've got time," he said, dropping the telegram on his desk and leaning back in his chair. He invited Laura to sit, and I remained standing.

I explained it all to him, and then finished by telling him that I had persuaded Kennedy and Martinez to work together to stop the rustling.

"Why didn't you come to me with this before?" he asked.

"I didn't know if I could trust you," I told him, honestly.

"Then you were out at that arroyo when those two men were killed?"

"I was," I admitted. "I killed Fred, but someone else cut Dobbs down before he could tell me what I needed to know about the rustlers."

He regarded me critically for a moment, then said, "You realize I could slap your ass in a cell right now and hold you for a judge?"

"I realize it," I said. "But I'm trusting you, Sheriff, to do the right thing."

"Yeah," he drawled, "the right thing."

He took some time to think it over, picking the telegram up from his desk several times, then dropping it back down again.

"All right, Adams, I'll go along."

"Thank you, Sheriff," Laura said. She hadn't had to say much to help me convince him, just the fact that she was there lent some credence to my words.

"Can you ride out to the ranch with us now?" I asked.

"I don't see why not," he said. "I can get a deputy—"

"No deputy," I said, quickly, "not yet."

"I was going to say that I can get a deputy to cover for me while I go with you," he said.

I held up my hands and said, "Sorry."

He nodded, then stood up.

"Why don't you get a drink or something. I'll meet you out front in half an hour."

"Okay," I said, and Laura stood up. "Thanks, Sheriff."

"You could still end up in jail, Adams," he said, keeping a handle on who was boss. I let him think what he liked.

"I know, Sheriff. I appreciate what you're doing."

"Sure. See you shortly."

We left his office and Laura said she wanted to check on something she had ordered in one of the stores.

"A dress," she said.

"All right. I'm going to the saloon. I'll meet you out here in twenty minutes or so."

"Okay."

She went off to her store and I walked to the saloon.

"Well, well," Bill said when he saw me, "I thought you were either gone or dead. Glad to see I was wrong on both counts."

"How you doing, Bill. Can I get a beer?"

"Sure thing." He brought the beer and asked, "What have you been up to?"

"Making friends," I said.

"Yeah?" he said, leaning his elbows on the bar. "What kind of friends?"

"You've got a dirty mind," I told him.

He leered at me and said, "Yeah!"

"Not those kinds of friends, Bill," I said. "I've settled my differences with people like Sheriff Cross, and old man Kennedy."

"Oh, yeah? No one's going to be taking shots at you anymore?"

"I hope not."

"Well, I'm for that. Beer's on the house, and let's hope there's no more lead headed your way."

I raised the mug and said, "Thanks. I'll drink to that."

I nursed a second beer and shot the breeze with him for a while, then when it was time to leave I said, "Got some things to do, Bill."

"Sure. You going to be in town much longer?"

Because of his question, I made a spur of the moment decision.

"Probably not more than another day," I lied. "I've had just about enough of this town."

"I know what you mean," he said. "Well, stop in and say goodbye if you get a chance."

"I will," I promised. "If I don't, take care of yourself."

We shook hands and I left.

I had decided at that moment to make it look as if I

were leaving town. The next morning I'd pack my rig and make a show of driving through town on my way out, and then I would double back to the Kennedy ranch and hide out there. With me out of the way, the rustlers might just feel good enough to try another illegal round up, and we'd have our chance to catch them in the act.

Maybe I wouldn't be around Lansdale, or the Kennedy ranch, for that much longer, after all.

If things worked out right.

40

When I got back to the sheriff's office, both Cross and Laura were waiting for me. Each stood by his horse, and it looked as if they hadn't spoken while they waited. We mounted and headed for the Kennedy ranch.

"Martinez was wondering why the Sheriff at Toro Rojo hadn't found the tracks that I found," I mentioned to Cross. Laura was riding up ahead of us.

"Is that your way of asking me why I never found any tracks on this side of the river?" he asked.

"Just making conversation, Sheriff," I told him.

He let it lie there for a while, then picked it up a couple of miles later, brushed it off, and gave me an answer.

"I've got a lot to do in Lansdale, Adams," he said. "It's a pretty big town."

"Yeah."

"Maybe I just never got out to the river in time to find any tracks. Maybe I had too many things to do, and by the time I did get out there, the tracks were gone."

"Yeah," I replied, "maybe." Only, with Enoch Kennedy being the important man he was, and with Cross supposedly "looking out for his interests," I couldn't believe that he wouldn't get right out there and look tracks, or some sign that would help clear up the rustling.

"You thought he was doing it, didn't you?" I asked.

"What?"

"You really thought that Kennedy was having his men rustle Martinez's cattle. That's why you never mentioned anything about finding tracks."

He didn't answer, just kept staring straight ahead at Laura's back.

"You did find tracks," I went on, "and they led right to the Kennedy herd, so you simply decided not to mention it to anybody. Isn't that right?" I asked.

He didn't answer.

"After all, part of your job was to look out after Kennedy's interests."

"That's right," he said. "Enoch Kennedy's interests. Suppose I did tell someone about what I'd found, suppose I did nail Kennedy himself for rustling. Where would that leave me, Adams?"

"Out of a job?" I asked.

"You're damn right. Kennedy backed me, and that made winning the election easy. Without his backing, what do you think would happen at the next election?"

"I think you're wrong, Sheriff," I replied. "I think you're running yourself down needlessly. From what I've heard, you've been a good lawman, and people wouldn't forget that."

"Sure, but people think what they want to think. Look what you thought. Kennedy backed me, so I was in Kennedy's pocket. Don't you think there are others who think that way? Sure, I looked out for the old man. I owed him that much, but I wasn't in his pocket."

"I'm sorry," I said, lamely.

"Don't be sorry, Adams," he said. "I'd probably think the same."

He wasn't in Kennedy's pocket, but he looked the other way when he thought Kennedy was breaking the law. Maybe he thought it was all right because Kennedy was simply retaliating against Martinez.

I put the question to him.

"Sure," he answered. "I figured they were just taking cows from each other, so who was losing out?"

"Well, I believe that neither man was involved," I said.

"That's why I'm out here with you, isn't it? So you can convince me?"

"That's why you're here," I said.

We rode the rest of the way in silence. Out of habit, I never let Cross end up riding behind me. He was always either between Laura and me, or ahead of both of us.

"Clint, sooner or later Bronson's got to find out that you're on the ranch," Laura said. "What's going to happen then?"

"We'll just have to do our best to keep him from finding out."

Which moving my rig from town to the ranch would make even harder to do. Maybe that was a mistake.

I asked Laura if she knew where we could hide my rig, so that when I left town it would also look as if I had left the area completely.

"There's the old barn."

"What old barn?"

"Well, when the house was first built we had another barn. It caught fire a few years later, and instead of knocking it down and rebuilding, father chose to build a totally new barn where it now stands."

"Where's the old one?"

"Behind the house a ways," she replied. "It's partially covered by brush and weeds, now, but it's there."

"Well, maybe we can get my rig into there," I proposed.

"If you leave town early enough tomorrow morning, I can bring you to the ranch in a roundabout way, avoid most of the men, and hopefully, avoid Deke."

"We'll give it a try, then," I said, and she nodded.

When we reached the house, Enoch Kennedy was waiting out front.

"Where's Bronson?" I asked.

"I sent him to the North ridge," he replied. "I told him that I had heard of some strays up there."

"Who did he take with him?" I asked.

"Vern Jory and Clete Smith, and some of the others."

"Any of those others show up on your list?" I asked him.

"No," he said, but he received little satisfaction from that fact. He turned to Cross and said, "Amos, thanks for coming."

"I'm willing to be convinced by what Adams has said, Mr. Kennedy," Cross said from astride his horse.

"This meeting should accomplish something," Kennedy said.

"Let's get going, then," I suggested.

Kennedy mounted up and we headed for the arroyo where I'd met Bronson and killed Fred.

I hoped nobody would end up dead this time around.

41

We got to the arroyo first and dismounted.

"I hope you were right to trust that girl," Laura said, digging at Lita even though the Mexican girl was not there.

"She'll bring him," I said, with more confidence than I felt.

Kennedy and Cross each found a rock to sit on and lapsed into conversation. I walked the arroyo about a hundred feet in each direction, checking behind any rocks that might be large enough to hide a man.

"Nervous?" Laura asked.

"Careful," I said.

Suddenly we heard the sounds of approaching horses and all looked up. There were three of them: Victor Martinez, Lita, and the sheriff, Roberto Aguilar.

When they reached us and dismounted it felt like an impending battle.

Kennedy and Martinez were exchanging wary gazes.

Aguilar and Cross were studying each other like two fighting cocks.

Lita and Laura were exchanging looks that could kill.

I stood in the middle, keeping them all apart. "Why don't we all get comfortable?" I suggested.

Everyone else found a rock while I remained standing.

"The point of this meeting is to devise an end to the rustling problem that has been plaguing both the Kennedy and Martinez ranches. Up until now, the general thinking has been that the two ranches have simply been stealing horses from each other. I don't believe that's the case."

"I have stolen nothing," Martinez confirmed.

"Neither have I," Kennedy said.

"And I believe both of you. I believe there is a third party who has been stealing stock from both of you, knowing you would each blame the other. I know who some of the men involved are. Bronson and Esteban are involved. They have to be, the arrangement wouldn't work if they weren't. I've told you all how I've come to these conclusions, now we have to catch them in the act, and hope that we can determine who is directing them."

"First, we must all accept your explanations," Aguilar said.

"Very well. Who does not accept it?" I asked.

I looked at all of them.

"Victor," Kennedy said, "I swear, I have never instructed my men to cross the border and steal your cattle, even though I did believe that you were stealing mine."

"Nor have I ordered your stock to be stolen, Enoch," Martinez answered. "It seems we have both been duped."

"Cross, Aguilar?" I said. "As long as they accept my explanation, what about you?"

"I'll go along," Cross said, "until I see some physical evidence to the contrary."

"I too will . . . go along, then," said the man with the patch.

The women remained silent and continued to exchange malevolent looks.

"All right, then. What we have to do is be there when they strike next," I said.

"How do we know where and when that will be?" Cross asked.

"I think we know where. The last place they hit was the Kennedy spread. I think that means they'll hit the Martinez ranch next. When? That's a problem, but I think I've figured out a way to push them into it."

"How?"

"I've been on the mind of the man who is behind all of this. I'm going to make it look as if I've left town, left the area altogether. With me gone, maybe they'll figure that it's safe to strike again."

"Makes sense, I guess," Cross commented.

Amos Cross was a smart lawman, with a mind of his own. The man with the patch, however, was Martinez's nephew. He was more of a puppet than Cross could ever imagine himself to be. He sat there, looking bored, offering no suggestions, no replies. He would do whatever his uncle told him to do.

"When will still be a problem, will it not?" Martinez asked.

"It will. We'll have to assemble some kind of a force, made up of men we can trust. Mr. Kennedy has already made a list of men he feels he can trust. Señor Martinez, I ask you to do the same."

"As soon as I return to my rancho."

"Continue to allow your foreman to place the guards on your herds. In addition, we will place our own guards to watch their guards."

"For how long?" Aguilar asked.

"For as long as it takes. We'll camp in the hills behind the Martinez herd if we have to. When they hit next, I want to be there, and I want representatives of both the Mexican and Texas law."

"I'll deputize you," Cross said.

"No," I said. I had reasons for not wanting to wear a badge again that I didn't want to go into at the moment.

"You have a deputy, don't you, Cross?" I asked.

"Yes."

"Can you trust him?"

"Yes."

"All right. Aguilar, have you a deputy?"

"No. Toro Rojo is a small town."

"All right, then. Since we expect them to hit in Mexico, you'll have to stay on the herd."

"All night, do you mean?" he asked.

"Roberto," Martinez growled, and the man with the patch fell silent. He was no doubt disturbed that he would have to do some actual work over the next few days—or weeks.

"I'll be pulling out of town tomorrow. Laura has given me a place where I can hide my rig and horse."

"Where will you be staying?" Martinez asked.

"At the Kennedy ranch." ·

"That will be cozy," Lita remarked.

"At least, my gear will be there," I added. "I'll be up in the hills with your men," I said to both ranchers, "watching the Martinez herd."

"I can't be there all the time," Cross said.

"Split the time between yourself and your deputy. As long as one of you is there, we'll have the authority we need."

"When do we grab them?" Cross asked.

"We'll show ourselves when they're in a vulnerable position," I said. "When there's less of a chance that they'll put up a fight."

"Where?"

They were all looking at me, waiting for the answer.

"Right in the middle of the Rio Grande."

42

Three days of camping in the hills behind Martinez's ranch had us all grating on one another's nerves.

"This is starting to look like it wasn't such a good idea," Amos Cross said. He was chewing on a piece of beef jerky. We had agreed in the beginning that we would not risk lighting a fire, so that meant no hot food, and no coffee.

I chewed on my own leathery jerky and said, "We knew it might take awhile, Cross."

"Yeah."

With us were five men from the Kennedy ranch, and four from Martinez's ranch. Also Aguilar, who proved to be worthless. All he did was bitch and sleep. After a while, we stopped complaining about his sleeping because at least that way he stayed quiet.

Laura and I were pretty sure we had succeedcd in hiding my rig and horses in the old, burnt-out barn without Bronson or any of his men seeing us.

Kennedy had his men picked out, and when Martinez picked his I told them not to mention anything to them. The first thing I wanted them to be told was to mount up and meet me in the hills behind the Martinez ranch—immediately. Just to be on the safe side, I didn't want any of them talking before they left.

Undoubtedly, there would be some grousing from the men, so I told both Kennedy and Martinez to offer them bonuses. That should have limited the complaining to barely audible whispers among themselves.

"Cup that cigarette," I told one of the men now, a Mexican who gave me a sour look and put the cigarette out instead.

"Go easy, Adams," Cross told me.

"Okay," I said.

From where we were we could see the Martinez herd and the men that Esteban had delegated to guard it. There was no sign of Esteban so far, but during the last two nights we knew he'd put in an appearance.

"What happens if the foreman discovers some of his men missing?" Cross asked. "From either ranch."

"They'll be told the men were sent somewhere by Kennedy or Martinez. If the foreman asks questions, there'll be a subtle reminder of who the boss is, and that will be that."

"We hope," Cross said. "I'd hate to be spending all of this time up here for nothing."

"So would I, but we've got a ways to go before we make that kind of a decision."

"Not that long," he said.

"It could be weeks, Cross," I reminded him.

"For you, maybe," he said. "Maybe you're prepared to stay up here for a few weeks, but I'm not. Nobody tried to shoot me, I don't have that incentive."

"No, I guess you don't," I remarked.

"If you're wrong, if Kennedy or Martinez, or both of them, really are stealing cattle, then they're down there laughing their heads off while we sit up here, the butt of their jokes."

"I don't think that's the case."

"It's a possibility."

"It's also a possibility that you could be involved, and you're sitting up here with me, laughing on the inside and crying on the outside."

"Or you," he said.

"Or one of them," I said, jerking my head at the men.

"There are a lot of possibilities," he said.

"Mine is the best, though," I said.

"Unless it proves to be a bust."

"Let's wait and see," I proposed, which put us right back where we started from, but at least the debate had helped to pass the time.

Two more nights went by without incident. I spent one of them with Cross's deputy, and on the fifth night Cross returned.

"Things are hopping in town," he told me that night. "I can't put up with this much longer."

"Hire more deputies," I suggested.

"Nobody wants the job."

"Why are you so anxious to chuck this in?" I asked.

"Maybe I haven't got your patience," he said. "Maybe I'm tired of staying up all night, listening to him snore," he added, indicating the sleeping Aguilar with a nod of his head.

I was looking down at the herd and noticed a change from the previous nights.

"Well, wake him up then," I told Cross, watching intently, "I think something's about to happen."

Cross looked down at the herd. "What are they doing?"

Three or four men were riding through the herd, and it soon became apparent what they were doing.

"Cutting the herd," I said.

"What?"

"They're separating some cows from the herd," I explained. "It looks like this is what we've been waiting for. Wake Aguilar and tell the men to get ready. When they start moving the cows to the river, we'll follow them."

Cross shook Aguilar, who didn't wake gracefully. He grunted and snorted, and Cross told him to shut up. He went about alerting the rest of the men while I continued to watch the activity down below.

"How many are they taking?" Cross asked.

"Looks to be about fifty, so far," I said. Another man came riding up, and I recognized him.

"Look," I said, "there's Esteban."

"And how many men?" Cross asked.

"They're still separating cows," I said, "but it looks like there's about five—six, with Esteban."

"Is that enough to drive the number of cows they're taking?"

"They could handle it," I said, "but if we get lucky, Bronson and some of his men will meet them."

"Hopefully at the border," he said. "If we're going to take them in the river, it won't do any good if Bronson is waiting for them somewhere on the Texas side."

"The cows will probably change hands at the river," I said. "They're getting them ready to move. Let's mount up."

"Why don't I ride and tell the Patron what is happening?" Aguilar asked anxiously.

"No way, Roberto," I told him. "We'll need you at the border to make the arrests."

He made a face and mounted his horse.

"There's something else I find strange here," Cross said to me.

"What's that?"

"Well, on the last incident on this side of the border, a man was killed."

"It could have been an accident, or maybe he got in the way and wasn't part of the set up."

"Well, there's still the fact that Bronson hates Mexicans, all Mexicans. Why would he team up with them?"

"He's not the man in charge, Cross. He's acting under orders, and if the man says he has to work with Mexicans, he doesn't have to like it."

"I suppose."

"They're moving off. Who's got that torch?"   .

"I have," one of Martinez's men called out.

"Keep it ready," I told him.

After the third night, I had thinned out the force of men that we kept on the hill to myself, Aguilar, Cross or his deputy, and Martinez's men. I had decided to leave Kennedy's men on the Texas side of the border. I figured once we started following the rustlers, we could figure out what general area of the river they would cross. I'd send one man ahead, and he would signal the men on the other side with the torch so they could get into position on the Texas side. Once the men and the cows were in the water, we would have them caught in a crossfire.

"Let's go," I said.

We had given the men and cows time to move off, and now we started after them.

"I guess you were right, Adams," Cross conceded as we rode along.

"Half right, anyway," I said. "We know that Esteban and some of his men are rustlers. Now we need Bronson and his boys."

"And the man in charge."

"Yes," I agreed, touching my gun. "And the man in charge."

43

Progress was slow and some of the men were starting to get impatient.

"Why don't we take them now, the cabrones," one of Martinez's men said aloud. "We should kill them for stealing from the Patron."

Some of the men agreed, angrily.

"We'll take them as planned," Cross spoke up, "and we'll take them alive, if possible." As he said this he nudged Aguilar with his elbow, who started, as if he had been dozing in his saddle.

"That is right," he said, and then his eyes half closed again. It was amazing to me that a man could look so formidable and prove so useless.

"Let's keep our voices down," I said, and everyone lapsed into silence.

"Señor," a man called out after a few moments had passed.

"Yes?"

One man rode up next to me, and I recognized him as a man named Carlos.

"What is it, Carlos?"

"I believe I know which part of the river they are going to," he said. "It is shallow there. A man could ride across without getting his knees wet."

"Cross?"

"Yeah, I think I know where he means. There are a few such areas up and down the river, but only one within an easy ride of here."

"All right, Carlos," I said. "Take the torch and circle around. Beat them to the border."

"Si, Señor. Pedro," he said to the man with the torch, who handed it over to him.

"Carlos, remember. Keep the signal short. We don't want the wrong people seeing it."

"Si, Señor. Good luck, Señor."

"You too, amigo," I said.

He left us and we continued the slow march to the border behind Esteban and the stolen cows.

Cross looked up into the sky and said, "Full moon. At least we'll have some light."

"More as it reflects off the water," I added, and he nodded.

We rode on in silence, and then Cross said, "We're getting close."

"Let's hope Kennedy's men saw the signal and are in position," I said.

"And that Bronson and his men didn't see it," Cross replied.

Finally, we came to within sight of the river and I told the men, "Spread out. Don't fire unless they do."

They were nervous now, and guns were drawn. I hoped they would be able to follow instructions.

"Aguilar!" I snapped.

"Eh?" he asked, looking around to see who called him.

"Roberto, you'll have to call out to the Mexicans. Tell them they're under arrest and to throw down their weapons."

"As you wish," he said in a resigned tone.

"Cross—"

"I know what to do," he said.

"Okay. Let's move closer. Don't do anything until I give the word."

As the Mexicans approached the river bank with the cows, a group of men appeared on the Texas side. The river was wide at this point, but there was still a chance the front end of the small herd would be out of the water before the stragglers were in. Some of the men might be on solid ground, but most of them would be in the water.

"Bronson," Cross said, looking across the river.

"Yeah. He's going into the water to meet them halfway," I said.

We watched as the Mexicans herded the cows into the water, and the Americans waded in to meet them. I heard somebody cock the hammer on their gun and I said, "Don't move until most of them are in the water."

Eventually, the tail end of the herd entered the water and all the Mexicans were in the Rio Grande. Up ahead, a few cows were coming out of the water with one or two of the Americans.

"Now!" I said.

We burst into the open and rode up to the river bank.

"Aguilar!" I said.

I'll give him this, he had a loud, commanding voice. He called out in Spanish. I saw the heads of the men in the water turn.

"My turn," Cross said, and then he called out.

"Bronson, you and your men are under arrest! You're trapped in the water! Throw down your weapons!"

I saw Bronson at the head of the small herd. His horse's front hoofs were barely in the water. He stood up in his stirrups and looked across at us. Then he looked behind him, and saw a group of Kennedy's men, who had responded to Carlos's signal. At that point Carlos rode up on us and I clapped his shoulder. He smiled and took his gun from his holster.

"Bronson!" Cross called again, and Aguilar chimed in with, "Esteban!"

The men in the water were looking around in confusion, waiting for someone to take charge and tell them what to do.

"Adams!" Bronson called out. "You out there Adams?"

"I'm here, Bronson," I answered.

"You're a dead man, Adams," he called. "Even if you get us, the Teacher will get you. You're a dead man."

And then he started firing, and all hell broke loose.

The men in the water took that as a sign to draw their guns and begin firing. To my left, Carlos grunted and fell from his saddle, dead or wounded.

"Fire!" Cross shouted.

We returned fire from our side, while Kennedy's men returned from the Texas side.

"Bronson!" Cross shouted, and I looked across the river. Bronson had broken to his left and was galloping along the bank of the Rio Grande. When he got far enough I knew he'd turn left and head into Texas.

"I'll get him," I shouted, and I took off along the bank on my side. When I got out of range of the firing, I'd cross and head after him.

The cows in the water were crying out loudly in confusion, and floundering in the water. If they'd been on dry ground they would have stampeded by now, and if the shooting went on any longer, they could still stampede. I had to leave them to Cross, though. I wanted Bronson. He had called the head man the "Teacher," and I was sure only he or Esteban would know who the Teacher was.

I had already seen Esteban blown out of his saddle in the midst of the gunfire, so Bronson was my only hope of finding the head man. The Teacher.

44

He had a good head start on me. Crossing the river had slowed me down, but once Duke was on dry land he started eating up the ground with those big strides of his. We were too far from the ranch and town for Bronson to outrun Duke, no matter how much horse he had under him, and the moon was bright enough so that I could make out his silhouette ahead of us.

Pretty soon we were close enough to Bronson for him to feel Duke's breath on the back of his neck. Before long I could read the panic on his face every time he turned around to check on my progress. He started to fire at me, but sitting on a moving horse is not an ideal shooting position.

When his gun was empty, he really started to panic. In minutes he was only a couple of lengths ahead and I could hear him breathing raggedly.

"Pull up, Bronson!" I called out. He kept riding. I drew my gun and fired over his head. He kept riding, and I saw him draw his rifle, which didn't worry me. It was even harder to fire a rifle accurately from a moving horse.

In moments I was alongside him and he stared at me in panic. He started to swing his rifle around, either to fire it at me or use it as a club, but I planted my boot in his side and shoved. He went flying off his horse and I pulled Duke up. Bronson's horse kept on going and I turned Duke around and rode back to where he lay on the ground. His rifle was about five feet from him, a desperate lunge away.

I stopped Duke and stared down at him. He was on his knees, about to get to his feet.

"Take it easy, Bronson," I told him.

He looked up at me and started to go for his revolver.

"It's empty, remember?"

His eyes flickered and he dropped his hand. Then he looked over at the rifle and started thinking about making that lunge.

"Go ahead, jump for it," I told him, leaning on the pommel of my saddle. "You'll be jumping right into hell."

"You won't be far behind, Adams. The Teacher will see to that."

"Yeah? Well then, why don't you tell me who this Teacher is, and I'll go and give him his chance. What do you say?"

He laughed nervously, still eying that rifle.

"The Teacher'll find you when he's ready, Adams. You busted up his operation. He ain't gonna like that."

"That's tough."

"You'll find out how tough," he said.

I watched while he mulled over his chances of making it to the rifle before I killed him.

"Go ahead, Bronson, go for it," I invited.

"You kill me, you'll never find the Teacher," he said.

"Nah," I told him. "I already know who he is. Go ahead, try for it."

"Whataya mean, you already know? How could you?"

"His name, once you think about it, it's a dead give-away. Now go for the rifle."

"You'll kill me."

"I'll kill you, anyway."

"No you won't. Not while I ain't armed."

"You got a gun in your holster."

"It's empty."

"Now, how was I supposed to know that?"

"You can't."

"Bronson," I said, "that's the rifle you used to put a hole in my shoulder, isn't it?"

The look in his eyes told me I got that one right.

"And you set me up at the arroyo to be killed, and then killed Dobbs before he could talk."

Again, the flicker of truth in his eyes, highlighted by the moonlight.

"You've been trying to make things uncomfortable for me since I got here," I told him, which was understating the matter.

His eyes flicked to the rifle again, and he wet his lips.

"Go ahead, Bronson. It's a short jump. You can make it—or would you like me to turn my back. Would that make you braver?"

He nailed me with a hard stare, and then he let out a war yell and jumped for the rifle.

I sent him to hell.

45

By daylight, Cletus Smith and some of the other boys from the Kennedy ranch were in the Lansdale jailhouse. Vern and a couple of others were dead. Esteban was dead, too, but the rest of his men were in the Toro Rojo jail.

Martinez and Lita came to the Kennedy house, and I said goodbye to them there.

"Señor Adams," Martinez said, "I am very grateful. You are welcome in my house always."

"Thank you," I said.

"Come, Lita. We go home."

Lita paused, though, and turned to me. "Won't you spend one more night with us?" She smiled seductively.

"I have to be moving on, Lita. I've been in this place too long."

"Will you come back and visit sometime?"

"Maybe," I said. "Sometime."

She touched my arm, smiled, and then followed after her father. Kennedy came out of the house with Laura as they were riding away.

"Mr. Adams, I can't thank you enough," he said, putting out his hand. I shook it and he said, "I'm glad you don't hold a grudge for some of the harsh things I've said to you."

"I never hold grudges, Mr. Kennedy," I told him. "I make promises, and I keep them."

"Yes, I see. Like your promise to find the man behind all the rustling. Won't you stay here until you do?"

"Him? I've already found him," I answered.

"You have?" he asked, surprised.

"Oh, yeah. After I've made my statement to Sheriff Cross, I'll take care of him just before leaving town."

"I see. Well, I wish you luck, then. That's a great load off my mind. Who is he, by the way?"

"Cross will tell you, after I'm done," I said. "Goodbye, Mr. Kennedy."

"Goodbye."

Laura had my wagon brought around, and now she was waiting for me by it.

"I wish you could stay one more night," she said.

"I can't," I said. I didn't elaborate, and she didn't ask again. I guess it stuck out all over me that I had the itch to be going.

"I heard what you told Father. Why don't you forget about the man and just leave?"

"He's the one I wanted from the beginning," I told her. "He's the reason I stuck around as long as I did. You heard me tell your father that I keep my promises. I meant it."

"Yes, I know you did." She put her arms around my neck and kissed me warmly, the kind of kiss that would have made another man stay. "Take care, Clint, and come see us."

"Goodbye, Laura."

I got up on my rig and headed for Lansdale, to keep my promise.

Back East, where I want to school, I had learned always to keep my promises. Especially to a Teacher.

46

After I made my statement to Cross, he asked me if I was headed out of town.

"Got one more stop to make," I told him.

"Where?"

"The saloon, for a farewell drink."

"Never thought you'd leave without finding the guy who set this all up," he said, eying me warily.

"Esteban and Bronson were probably the only ones who knew who he was, and they're dead."

"Yeah, still—"

"So long, Sheriff. I'll try not to visit your town again."

"I'll take that as a promise."

I didn't tell him how I felt about promises, I just waved and left his office.

I didn't want to tell Cross that I knew who the Teacher was. I didn't want him putting him behind bars before I had a chance to talk to him.

I drove my rig up in front of Bill Chambers's saloon. Before getting down I unbuttoned the two bottom buttons of my shirt, and then I went into the saloon.

"Hey, Clint. How goes it?" Bill asked from behind the bar.

"Great, Bill. Get me a beer, will you?"

"Sure." He brought it over and said, "I thought you left town days ago."

"That's what everybody was supposed to think. We wanted the rustlers to make another try, and they did, last night."

"Yeah? What happened?"

"We got them all," I said, after a mouthful of beer. "Some dead, but most of them in jail."

"Got them all, huh? That's good, that's what you wanted, right?"

"That's almost what I wanted," I replied. "The only thing left is the man who was in charge, the man who gave the order for me to get shot."

"Who's that?"

"They called him the Teacher."

"Funny name," he said.

"You ought to know, Bill. You picked it," I said, catching his eyes and holding them with mine.

"What are you talking about?"

"I'm talking about a man, an educated man, who thought he could be satisfied with a simple life, and then found out he couldn't. He cooked up a scheme, hooked a couple of ambitious foremen into it, and then had them recruit some others. They were the only ones who knew who he really was, though. To the rest of the men he was known only as the Teacher."

"So? What's that got to do with me?" he asked. He had both hands beneath the bar now and I watched his eyes.

"You used to be a teacher, Bill," I said.

"Come on, Clint. There's other teachers in town, ain't there?"

"Sure," I said. "A little old lady of sixty. I think we can count her out, Bill. No, you're it. You're smart enough to have thought of it, and you kept a low profile and let Bronson and Esteban do all the work. You got most of the profits, though, from selling the stolen cows, and it was a hell of a lot more than you make out of this place."

"This place," he said, in disgust. "This place is a shithouse. Keep your right hand on the bar, Clint. I got a scattergun under here, and it'll shoot right through."

"You're the boss, Teacher," I said.

"Now, reach over with your left hand, unbuckle your belt and let it drop."

I did as he said.

"Now, back away from the bar."

Backing away I said, "You going to blow me apart with that shotgun, Bill? How you going to explain that?"

"Everybody out!" he shouted, suddenly. "Everybody" was about five men, and Bill told them he was closing up. If they were curious about me and why I'd dropped my gunbelt, they kept it to themselves. They couldn't see Bill's hands, and they probably hadn't heard anything we said. They did as he said, and filed out.

We were alone.

"I'll think of a story, don't you worry," he said, answering my last question.

"Yeah," I said, "I'll bet you will. If you kill me, Enoch Kennedy's going to be awful mad."

"Why's that?" he asked. He was interested because if he intended to keep living in Lansdale—providing his story held up, that is—it wouldn't pay to be on Kennedy's wrong side.

"Well, this town is his best kept secret," I explained. "You kill me, the Gunsmith, and you're going to put this town on the map for sure."

That made him think. I lowered my hands slowly, and when he wet his lips I went for the hideaway .22 New Line in my belt. At the same time I moved, he triggered the shotgun. The front of the bar exploded out, showering wood splinters and metal pellets. If I'd been farther away, the pellets might have spread out enough to catch me, but that close they stayed bunched and missed me completely.

Then I pulled the trigger of the .22 three times, and kept my promise.

THE END

WESTERNS

Nelson Nye

☐ 14199	**DEATH VALLEY SLIM** $1.95	
☐ 30798	**GUN FEUD AT TIEDOWN/ROGUES RENDEZVOUS** $2.25	
☐ 37343	**IRON HAND** $1.95	
☐ 80576	**THEIF RIVER** $1.95	
☐ 52041	**THE MARSHAL OF PIOCHE** $1.95	
☐ 58376	**THE NO-GUN FIGHTER** $1.95	

Double Westerns

☐ 04731	**BANCROFT'S BANCO/SEVEN SIX-GUNNERS** $2.25

Available wherever paperbacks are sold or use this coupon.

J. R. ROBERTS

THE GUNSMITH

SERIES

An all new series of adult westerns, following the wild and
lusty adventures of Clint Adams, the Gunsmith!

☐	30856	THE GUNSMITH #1: MACKLIN'S WOMEN $2.25
☐	30857	THE GUNSMITH #2: THE CHINESE GUNMEN $2.25
☐	30858	THE GUNSMITH #3: THE WOMAN HUNT $2.25
☐	30859	THE GUNSMITH #4: THE GUNS OF ABILENE $2.25
☐	30860	THE GUNSMITH #5: THREE GUNS FOR GLORY $2.25
☐	30861	THE GUNSMITH #6: LEADTOWN $2.25

Available wherever paperbacks are sold or use this coupon.

C ACE CHARTER BOOKS
P.O. Box 400, Kirkwood, N.Y. 13795

Please send me the titles checked above. I enclose $_____.
Include $1.00 per copy for postage and handling. Send check or
money order only. New York State residents please add sales tax.

NAME_____

ADDRESS_____

CITY_____STATE_____ZIP_____

C-03

Winners of the SPUR and WESTERN HERITAGE AWARD

Awarded annually by the Western Writers of America, the Golden Spur is the most prestigious prize a Western novel, or author, can attain.